This remarkable story (winner of the World Fantasy Award 1985 for the Best Novella) appeared first in a slightly shorter form in the science fiction magazine *Interzone* and has received extraordinary international praise.

This edition is the unique, full-length version of the story, complete with stunning line drawings throughout by artist Sacha Ackerman.

Geoff Ryman is the author of the award-winning novels THE WARRIOR WHO CARRIED LIFE and THE CHILD GARDEN.

THE UNCONQUERED COUNTRY

A Life History

Geoff Ryman

Illustrations by Sacha Ackerman

UNWIN
PAPERBACKS

LONDON SYDNEY WELLINGTON

First published in paperback by Unwin® Paperbacks, an
imprint of Unwin Hyman Limited in 1986
This edition, 1990

UNWIN HYMAN LIMITED
15/17 Broadwick Street
London W1V 1FP

Allen & Unwin Australia Pty Ltd
8 Napier Street, North Sydney, NSW 2060, Australia

Allen & Unwin New Zealand Pty Ltd with Port Nicholson Press
Compusales Building, 75 Ghuznee Street, Wellington,
New Zealand

The right of Geoff Ryman to be identified as author of this work
has been asserted by him in accordance with the Copyrights,
Designs and Patents Act, 1988.

British Library Cataloguing in Publication Data is available on
request

ISBN 0 04 440776 9

Printed in Great Britain by Cox & Wyman Ltd, Reading

for John Lennon,
for Philip K. Dick, for Walter

Sacha Ackerman was born in 1951 in the USSR and emigrated in 1973. His work has been exhibited in personal and group exhibitions in Israel, France and Switzerland. This is the first book that he has illustrated.

Contents

I watched a family of about eight persons – a man and a woman, both about fifty, with their children about one, eight and ten, and two grown-up daughters of about twenty to twenty-four. An old woman with snow white hair was holding the one-year-old in her arms and singing to it, and tickling it. The child was cooing with delight. The couple were looking on with tears in their eyes.

The father was holding the hand of a boy about ten years old and speaking to him softly; the boy was fighting his tears. The father pointed to the sky, stroked his head and seemed to explain something to him.

From the transcripts of the Nuremberg Trials
as reported in *The Quality of Mercy: Cambodia,
Holocaust and Modern Conscience*
by William Shawcross.

PART ONE

The New Numbers

THIRD CHILD had nothing to sell but parts of her body. She sold her blood. A young man with a cruel warrior's face – a hooked nose between two plump cheeks – came to her room every two weeks. He called himself her Agent, and told a string of hearty jokes, and carried a machine around his neck. It was rather like a pair of bagpipes, and it clung to him, and whimpered.

Third rented her womb for industrial use. She was cheaper than the glass tanks. She grew parts of living machinery inside her – differentials for trucks, small household appliances. She gave birth to advertisements, small caricature figures that sang songs. There was no other work for her in the city. The city was called Saprang Song, which meant Divine Lotus, after the Buddha.

When Third was lucky, she got a contract for weapons. The pay was good because it was danger-ous. The weapons would come gushing suddenly out of her with much loss of blood, usually in the middle of the night: an avalanche of glossy, freckled, dark brown guppies with black, soft eyes and bright rodent smiles full of teeth. No matter how ill or exhausted Third felt, she would shovel

3

Third and the yarrow numbers

them, immediately, into buckets and tie down the lids. If she didn't do that, immediately, if she fell asleep, the guppies would eat her. Thrashing in their buckets as she carried them down the steps, the guppies would eat each other. She would have to hurry with them, shuffling as fast as she could under the weight, to the Neighbours. The Neighbours only paid her for the ones that were left alive. It was piece work.

The Neighbours had coveted the lands of Third's people for generations. Then the people of the Big Country had, for reasons of their own, given the weapons to the Neighbours. Third's nation had called itself the Unconquered Country. It had never been colonised. When the Neighbours came, it fought. Third had been a child in a rebel village in the hills that had flown the white and yellow flag of the Unconquered People. The women had worked the rice, while the men kept watch in the hills, with old guns from other wars.

The name Third Child had been a spell, to make sure that there would be no more children born to her mother and father. The spell worked. A month after Third was born, her father was killed. By a tiger, it was said. There were very few tigers left. They had become beasts of portent. They ate people.

Third looked ordinary, to herself and others. She

5

loved numbers. Her cousin, who was a man, had a position as an Accountant. Third would sit next to him in rapt and silent wonder, as the yarrow stalks clicked back and forth, counting in fan-shaped patterns. Her cousin was charmed that she was interested, sweet and silent as a child should be. He showed her how the yarrow worked.

Numbers were portents too. They were used as oracles. This was a practical thing. Rice shoots were counted; yields were predicted; seed was stored. Numbers spread out in fan-like shapes, into the future.

Third could read them. She saw yarrow in her mind, ghost yarrow she sometimes called them, and they would scurry ahead of the real stalks. They moved too fast for her to follow, flashing, weaving. They leapt to correct answers, ahead of her cousin.

If anyone asked Third how much rice was in a bowl, she would answer 'enough'. It was always polite to answer that there was enough rice, even when there wasn't. But if anyone had pressed for more detail, Third could have answered '600 to 700 grains'. The yarrow stalks in her mind would click, telling her how much space ten grains took – as represented by so many lengths cut into a stalk – and how much space there was in a bowl. The ghost yarrow opened and closed, like a series of waving fans, beautiful, orderly, true.

As Third carried food to her mother in the fields, the yarrow would move. They told her the number of rice shoots, and the rate of their growth. She would have an early sense of the harvest, and how many days were left until they all could rest. She could not follow the waving fans, but she could feel her mind driving them. It was a pleasurable sensation, this slight sense of forcing something ahead. She could make them go faster if she wanted to.

It was how she saw the world; it was as if the world were a forest of yarrow, moving all around her, as if numbers were leaves, rustling in the wind.

Third did not talk much. This was considered delightfully demure. She helped around the house, she found helping about the house very easy, and even her mother, who was used to her, had to exclaim at the tidiness of Third. Her second sister was chagrined. But her eldest sister was proud of her. Everything was always tidy around Third. The mat, the vase, the wooden cup, the brazier, the clay pot full of sour sauce: they were in place. You knew Third had been at work because it was beautiful. Organised according to some unseen principle that even the number-blind could recognise as possessing quality.

'Our little princess', her eldest sister would call her. Only princesses in stories had time for arranging flowers. Third worked quickly. This house had no flowers, but it looked as if it did.

The rebels had an interest in education. They sent a teacher to Third's village, and she was a woman of great application. She stayed eight weeks and two days, and then she had to go back to the war. It would be, as one always had to say, enough.

She was to teach the children how to read and to count. Third was averagely bad at her letters. This was mostly due to shyness. To read, you had to stand and speak, and this she had never been called upon to do. The language of the People was not pictographic, but it was tonal and each sound-sign had to show shifts in tone. It was ferociously complicated. Third was interested in the architecture of the signs. Their shapes kept turning in her mind into proportions that as yet had no meaning. The teacher would force her to speak, to say something.

'I like that,' Third said, pointing to an arch in a sign and following it with her finger.

'But what does the sign sound like?' the teacher would insist.

Third would go quiet and downcast, feeling that she was doing wrong. The question made no sense. Sign sound like? A sign sounds? Small brown face and black button eyes were clouded with withdrawal and remorse.

Oh my People, the teacher would think, looking at her, despairing. There was so much to do. She could not be angry.

It was at mathematics that Third was noticeably backward. Numbers for her were always part of something else. They could only exist in relation to other numbers, in relation to real things. They could not be uprooted and made alone. They were related, like people.

'What number is this?' the teacher would ask, holding up a card.

'Number as what?' Third would murmur. She tried to read the digits as she read the yarrow. Their proportions carried no meaning.

'Number of anything,' the teacher would answer. 'Just the number. By itself.'

Third would stare back mournfully at her, and the teacher would pass on to another child. The teacher taught the children by day, under a screen of bamboo, so that they could not be seen from the air.

'One day,' she told them, 'the Neighbours will be gone. The Neighbours will be gone, and the foreigners will be gone, and the People will need to work, to build. You will have to build. You will have to work, to count, to read.'

What the People needed to be, what they had to become, were fighters. That was what the teacher knew. Third was self-contained, beautifully mute, as was expected of children of the People, and this made the teacher very impatient. The People must stop being quiet, to stay themselves, to hold back the Neighbours and the Big People, who wanted to swallow the Unconquered.

The teacher turned Third into a symbol. The symbol was this: when this one small girl learns to count, I will know I have done some good. Third became a target. It was a kind of love.

She made Third stay after the others. She held up cards. 'What number is this? What number is this, Third? Look. Tell me the number.'

Third, seized with a panic that she was doing wrong, would not move, would not speak. She had never done wrong, and her teacher was trying so hard, paying her special attention. And Third hated it. That made her feel even more in the wrong.

She went off at night, creeping out of her house, to pound the mud with her feet, and fling the yarrow stalks in her mind at the sky in anger, going over and over them, trying to find some link with the marks on the horrible cards. Even then, Third did not cry.

Then, one day, the teacher had an inspiration.

It was after class. The other children were back out in the fields, shaking the muddle out of their heads. Third was alone with the teacher again.

'Well,' the teacher said. 'Today we try a different approach.' And she brought out the yarrow stalks.

No, thought Third. Leave those alone.

'Now, Third, look. One. One stalk. Not many stalks. Just one stalk by itself,' said the teacher, and smiled, and watched. 'That is one.'

It was like a door beginning to open, and it was as if Third slammed it shut. Third was in terror, though she did not know why.

'Now, Third. Two. Two yarrow stalks.'

Lips pressed together, Third jammed all the stalks back together in a bunch.

'No, no. Two. See? Only two.'

Blindly this time, Third reached for the yarrow, and the teacher took hold of her hands, and pushed them away. She picked up the yarrow stalks and hid them behind her back. Third tried to reach round her, one quick, tiny hand after another. The teacher had to use both hands to fend her off. The yarrow were left behind her on the mat. Third sat back. The teacher relaxed. Third leapt forward, and grabbed a fistful of the yarrow, and the teacher laughed.

Third made a fan, one yarrow stalk between each finger. Still chuckling, shaking her head, the teacher grabbed the yarrow and used them as levers to prise apart Third's fingers.

'Sit there,' the teacher said, and pushed Third

11

back. 'Now. One. Two. Three.' She laid the stalks down, but far apart, in parallel lines that Third knew could never meet. Three. Three stalks together made three parts of a whole. These did not. Third understood, and she did not want to. As if tearing through flesh, the teacher was rending the numbers apart. She was making them alone.

Third turned and tried to run. The teacher yelped with laughter, and grabbed her, and hugged her, controlled her by hugging her.

'You won't get away that easily,' grinned the teacher.

Third wanted to hit her. She wanted to yell and scream and get away, but she could do none of those things. She was frozen. She was going to have to count.

'Give me numbers,' whispered the teacher.

'One ... two ... three,' Third said, looking down, in a tiny and wan little voice.

For some reason, the teacher was disappointed.

'Oh,' the teacher said, and dropped her arms, and gave Third a little pat. 'Good. That was simple, wasn't it? Now you can count. And after that is four and five.' The teacher laid down more stalks. 'See? Four and five. Say four and five, Third.'

'Four and five,' murmured Third, and everything around her seemed bated, like breath.

'Now say them all together, all the numbers.'

Let me go, Third's eyes pleaded, but the teacher pretended not to understand. The teacher kept it up, all the way to ten. In the end, it was the teacher who had to leave. Third was left alone, under the screen, quick night having fallen. She was afraid to move.

Something terrible had happened to the numbers. They wouldn't work. Third tried to drive the yarrow in her mind, but as soon as they touched on any one of the new numbers, they were snagged by something. They stopped, and had to start again, grew confused, or were left naked, hanging, and Third realised she had never really understood how they danced their way to answers. They were going away, like friends.

She walked to her cousin's house, taking tiny steps. She was frightened that if she ran, she would disturb the numbers more.

They were eating at her cousin's house, but Third gave no words of greeting and did not take off her shoes. She walked very carefully to her cousin, and dropped to her knees next to him and folded herself up into a tight, supplicant little ball. She was shaking.

'Third Child, cousin?' he asked alarmed, meaning what is wrong? He thought her mother had died.

'The numbers. The yarrow,' she said, her words like little parcels.

13

'Ah!' said her cousin, and began to smile.

'Show me how they work!'

'But you know how they work.' Third said nothing. Her cousin cradled her up next to him, and kissed her forehead, and held her to his plump bosom and his crisp plaid shirt. 'Your teacher,' he said, 'says I must not.'   —

He could feel her wilt.

'You will get used to the new numbers in time,' he cajoled her, shaking her slightly with affection. It was touching how important small things seemed to children. 'You will see. They are new, modern numbers, and we can use them to fight the Neighbours.' But his face was darkening, for under his hand, the child was trembling.

Third's eldest sister came looking for her. 'Little Princess!' she said in alarm. 'What has she done to you?' They began to understand that something had been broken.

Sometimes at night, the old numbers would return, like the ghosts they were. Like ghosts, they were disordered, limping. The things they whispered made no sense. They were sad in the way that ghosts are sad, trying to fight their way back to life, back to sense, irredeemably marred.

Third welcomed them, and hoped for them and wanted them to work. She pitied them, and finally, she grew weary of them. She could still use the real yarrow stalks as well as other children did. That was, after all, enough.

She did not remember the exact day that the teacher left. She only remembered the hateful nugget of gladness she felt when the teacher was gone. The teacher was going back to the war. When Third heard the teacher had been killed, she was glad.

There was the rest of the summer. It seemed a long time then. It rained. The marriage of Third's cousin was arranged. He would be wed after the monsoons, and Third would help with the flowers.

His family had a house-birthing for him. His new house was born, and was led baby-wet and making soft, breathy noises from house to house. It stumbled on its fat, dimpled white legs, and it wore strings of bangles as it was paraded. The People sang it songs, and patted it, and the children rode on its patient back. Third's cousin would train it as it grew, to shelter his new family.

The houses of the People were alive. They lived for generations, with wattles and wrinkles and patches of whisker, like ancient grannies. They wore roofed porches from their heads, like reed hats. They knew their families and cared for them. It was said that they remembered even those who had died long ago, and grieved for them. It was said

15

they had a special cry for the dead, to greet their family's ghosts.

Third was under her house when the Neighbours came. She was feeding the hens. In her language, hens were called Great Fat Ladies in White Bloomers. Third fed them slugs she had collected from the paddies. She counted their eggs and she knew which Ladies were fattest. She knew their future from their weight.

It was the first cloudless day. The old house above her sighed and shifted on its haunches. It fed on light. The borders of its shadow were sharply defined on the dust.

Suddenly there was a warbling. It was from the men on the hill, and the house stood up.

It lurched to its feet, swaying, and the wicker cages between its legs snapped and flew apart. There were crashes of falling crockery overhead. Third knew her second sister had been beside the charcoal stove. She heard her second sister scream. Third ran outside to see.

All along the valley, the houses began to hoot in panic. The flood warning, the warning for a flood, over and over. The hens scattered, in wavering lines.

Low overhead and silently, came Sharks. Sharks, it was said, had been human once. Sunlight reflected on their humming wings, and they were

16

long and sleek and freckled with big brown spots like old people get on their hands. Third saw their round and happy faces. She saw them smile. As they passed, wind whipped into her face, and she turned.

An attack. Third knew what to do in an attack. She was to hide in the deepest part of the house, and wrap herself in white blankets. But the porch of the house now towered above her head. Her sister stood on it, wailing, beetroot red, scalded by the stove.

'Sister get inside!' cried Third. The old house trumpeted with relief, and snatched Third up with its trunk. It thought there was a flood, thought it had to keep Third from trying to swim, from drowning, so it lifted her up high over its round and featureless head, and began to march for the higher ground. The ground was still moist. There was no dust. Third could see everything.

She saw the stampede of houses, as they gained speed, throwing their great feet forward into a lumbering trot, their heads bobbing with effort. She saw the fields beyond, the women running, but she could not see her mother, and she saw the Sharks. They puffed out their cheeks and they blew, and where they blew, everything died in a line, like a furrow.

The rice went brown, crumpling up like burning paper. A Great Fat Lady collapsed in a rumpled

17

The Sharks attack

heap like a balloon losing air, her feathers curling up, melting away. Third knew where the path of destruction was proceeding. She knew who was going to fall next, who was running to intercept the lines of death. She tried to call to them. 'Madame Goh! Madame Goh! Stop running!' she piped, and heard the frailty of her own voice. She looked for her mother. She looked for her sister.

The old guns on the hill leapt forward and settled back, and there was a boom and batter that made Third scream and cover her ears. Parts of the opposite hillside were thrown up as chunks of rock and the spinning heads of trees. The Sharks whistled, cheering, as if at a football match, and swept low over the guns. After that, the guns were silent. The Sharks rose up in the sky, reflecting light from their wings like dragonflies. They were almost beautiful for a moment. Then they turned and descended on the village. As they levelled out, Third knew she was directly in their path.

Third's eldest sister jumped down from her cousin's house as it lumbered forward. She dodged between the houses on her long stick legs, in her red gingham dress.

'House,' she called as she ran. 'Old house. Kneel down! Kneel down!'

She jogged backwards beside it, jumping up and down, trying to reach Third. The house was too panicked to notice, and Third was clogged with terror. Third saw the faces of the Sharks, the row of smiles, the number of teeth. They batted their eyelashes at her, and giggled. They puffed out their cheeks like the Four Winds, and blew.

Third turned her head, and felt the withering blast of anti-life pass her by. It scraped her ankle, and the flesh over the bone rose up in protest, bubbles of oil seething under a patch of skin. She felt the backwash of air as they passed. She felt a wing throb, almost gently for a moment, on the top of her head. There was tinkling, musical laughter, a sprinkle of notes that almost reassured Third Child. Then she looked down.

Her eldest sister lay in a puddle. The gingham dress had gone orange. Her skin was a sickly, translucent yellow, rucked up and crinkled and soft. Her pigtails had gone altogether; strands of hair blew in the dust.

Overhead, the Sharks made a rude, farting sound. They sashayed in the air, bumping their middles from side to side, as if they had hips. They were mocking humankind.

The Neighbours followed soon after, in the cavernous bellies of winged transports. There were ninety of them, in three parties. They did not look different from the Unconquered People. They had the same sleek brown skin and they were not ugly. They wore green coolsuits against the heat, and had bands of metal strapped to their index fingers that spurted fire and light where they pointed. They also carried the ceremonial bayonets that were the mark of a true warrior. The Sharks hovered overhead, holding the fluttering banners of the Neighbours in their teeth.

Third's mother sat in the darkest part of the house, Third and her second sister on her lap, rocking them, going 'Sssh, Ssssh, Sssh,' to soothe them. The eldest sister still lay in the dust outside: the second sister wailed, inconsolably. For Third everything was muffled, even the pain in her ankle. Third was silent. She must have gone for a drink of water, for at some point she was standing in front of the window by the tub. Through a wavering curtain of hot, rising air, she saw two village men being led out into the paddies. All the sound was muffled, too, except for the buzzing of flies.

One of the villagers was her cousin. He had a soft round face and a thick moustache. He wore a crisp plaid shirt that his mother would have beaten clean that morning, and the loose black leggings of the People. The trousers had had an airy slit up the inside leg, and one of the Neighbours ran the blade of his bayonet up along it. Her cousin stepped back, scowling, too anxious to be angry. Third saw one of the Neighbours tell a joke, laughing, and flick his cigarette into the water.

Both men were pushed down on to their knees. The other villager, a wiry and nervous uncle, began to plead, jabbering. A Neighbour knelt on his shoulder, and pulled his head back, hard, by the hair. The uncle held up the thin palms of his hands against the bayonets.

Third's cousin knelt, fists folded, calmly glancing over his shoulders at the familiar hills, as if he did not care about them, not yet sure, unable to believe, that he was going to die.

Third did not remember his murder. She remembered the face of the man who did it. He was tiny and thin and wretched, with outlines of gold around his tobacco-stained teeth. His cheeks were deeply scarred by pockmarks, and he was grinning a rictus grin. It took over the lower half of his face, and Third understood that he was grinning in order to frighten, because he felt evil, and he thought that this was what evil looked like, and that evil made him important.

Suddenly her cousin was on his side, his face still soft and confused. Once he and Third had gone out together to look at the stars, and he had lain on the ground like that. Third had fallen asleep with her head on his chest. Blood spread across his chest now, in the orderly patterns of the crisp plaid shirt.

The houses

He was the Accountant. No one else would know as well as he did how the yarrow worked. Third's mother eased her away from the window.

The Neighbours came for a visit. They took swigs of water from Third's cup. 'We are your friends,' they told Third's mother, and requisitioned the rice she had not hidden. They told her to save her menstrual blood. Third's mother dipped and bowed to them, hands high over her head. She smiled. When they were gone, she pulled Third to her, and hugged her, and her hands were trembling. Third listened to the Neighbours under her house, chasing her White Ladies. They were taking them away.

'They are going to do something with our blood,' said Third's mother. 'They want to weaken the male power of our men.'

They slaughtered ten of the old houses. Third's own house began to make a new noise, a wheedling noise, tightly constrained. The walls shook delicately. Third's mother risked looking out of the window, and saw them hacking at the carcass of their cousin's house. The new little white house lay by its side. The Neighbours began to erect new, dead houses that could not walk to other valleys.

'There is nothing for us here,' said Third's mother. In the night, she parcelled up the stove, and a pot, and their rice, and she led her children away from the village.

They had to leave their old caring house behind. They tethered it to a stake. It knew it was being left, and couldn't understand why. As they crept away it began to bellow after them, tugging at the line that held it. Deserted houses sometimes died of love.

'Go!' whispered Third's mother, and pushed her, and gave her another nudge when Third turned around. 'Keep going! Don't look back even if I fall down.' They heard the Neighbours call to each other. They sounded like dogs barking. Third and her family flitted into the shadow of the trees and waited until their house fell silent. Then they moved on.

They went, like everyone else, to the City. Third's mother carried them most of the way on her back.

There would have been flowers at the wedding of Third's cousin. Years later, she still found herself looking forward to it. All the village girls would have been linked together by a chain of flowers. Third would have tended the bride.

The villagers grew the flowers, lotuses, along the borders of the rice paddies. The flowers were not picked, except for special occasions. In the mornings the lotuses would be open wide; by noon they would be shut. There had been a medium in the village who claimed she had the soul of a prince who was in turn possessed by the soul of a sorcerer. Third had once seen her eat a glass cup to prove it, crunching it in her mouth. Each house had a shrine to the Buddha, which was exchanged each month with a different house.

The People sang when they spoke. The language was tonal; melody carried meaning. The numbers sang too. The yarrow would be cast into patterns that were tones. They seemed to speak. They turned into songs.

There were feast songs, work songs, cooking songs, cast by the yarrow. Everyone sang them. Long afterwards, Third would find herself humming them. She no longer knew what they meant. She had forgotten the words and the numbers. But they still murmured to her, like voices in memory.

Her name was a spell, a number, and Third's mother only had to say it, to remember tigers. As they fled from the village, Third and her family were in terror of tigers. Where they slept, Third's mother made a fire against them.

In the middle of the night, Third felt hot breath on her cheeks, and opened her eyes. Looming over her, as large as she was, was the face of the tiger. There was blood on its muzzle, and its great green eyes stared into her, piercing her like shafts, brush-

26

ing, it seemed, her very soul, making it go hushed and cold. Third did not move. There was nothing she could do. The tiger snuffled her once more and then, having eaten already, silently padded away on its big orange feet. Third looked, and saw that her mother and sister were still alive.

Third couldn't sleep after that, so she tried counting the stars. It was so slow. One. Two. Three.

Suddenly there was a great rising out of her of numbers. A rage of numbers, the old numbers, angry and dislocated. They reached up out of her for something, some answer, some reason. They almost seized it. The size of the world. The number of the People. Third felt her breath and heart constrict. The numbers withdrew like a flock of birds into the sky. She could almost hear them cawing. She saw the pattern they made. It was the pattern of the future, black wings and tiger stripes.

In the morning, she stood up when her mother did and told her nothing about it.

PART TWO

The Ceremony

THE CITY of Saprang Song had paved streets, over 2,000 of them, and plumbing, enough for a million people. By the time Third was an adult, eight million, half of the People, had crowded into it.

The old city was made of stone and steel: the new city was made of flesh. The Neighbours had introduced a new kind of mobile home. It was slow and stupid, a long beige tube, with ribs in its ceiling, and a single window, and a single door. When it was closed, the door looked like the bottom of a mushroom, all gills. When it opened, a flap of flesh came out like a tongue, steps to climb.

The houses were supposed to spread out, across the countryside. Instead, the refugees discovered that the houses could climb, on legs that looked like the cooked wings of chickens. They had long hairs like wires. The houses could cling to each other's backs. As the refugees swarmed, the houses rose up in haphazard towers, tall lopsided heaps of housing, waves of it, with no streets between them. They looked like a piled mass of conestoga wagons.

The People had to walk up and over each other's houses to get to their own, or squeeze through

31

The new city

narrow passageways past houses turned into tiny shops or brothels. They shouted at each other to be quiet, and fended off new, creeping houses with brooms. Lines of laundry, grey and faded, hung between the towers, and the air was always full of the smell of cooking and the hearty blare of media entertainment. Sometimes the ribs of the lowest houses would break from the weight, and the towers would collapse in a fleshy avalanche. In the monsoon rains, the water would drain down the towers in steps, like waterfalls, and flood the lowest layers. The houses would go diseased, soft and bruised and seeping. The very poorest people dried the dead ones, and lived in the husks. Or they ate them.

They fought with municipal beasts that prowled the streets eating garbage and the unloved dead.

Third was going to sell her left eye. It was common practice. There were dealers. They would prise it out of her, without any drugs for the pain, and freeze it, and sell it for transplants or machinery. It was illegal, of course. The dealers had stalls in the markets that could be moved quickly when the Neighbours came.

There were many people waiting in line. The old woman in front of Third already had a puckered pouch of skin where one eye should have been. She was going to sell her second eye in order to buy her

grand-daughter a wedding coat. She was very calm
and gracious and proud, in immaculate black. 'You
must not imagine I was always like this, oh no,' she
said smiling, wagging a finger. 'I was a high lady in
my village.' They all said that, but the gentle,
precise way she spoke made Third believe her.
'Now my grand-daughter will be one as well. That
is her mother, there, my daughter.' A woman in a
glossy pink jacket stood well away from the line,
pretending not to see them. 'Isn't she pretty? She is
so embarrassed. Make sure she gets the money,
please.'

'You. Next,' said the dealer, looking harassed and
chubby in his white shorts and bright printed shirt.
He led the old woman away with his young son to
help. He drew a black drapery on rings, like a
shower curtain, around her. When the old woman
emerged, both eyes were closed, and her skin was
white and greasy with sweat, and she reached out
into the air for Third, and tried to speak, but the
sound was slurred and distorted, like a tape at the
wrong speed. She grabbed Third's arm, and Third
felt a jolt from her, like electricity, from the quaking
of her bones.

Third fainted. She lacked food and blood, and
she'd been standing for hours, and waves of nausea
seemed to pour out of the old woman. When Third
awoke, on asphalt, on crushed and sour cabbage,

34

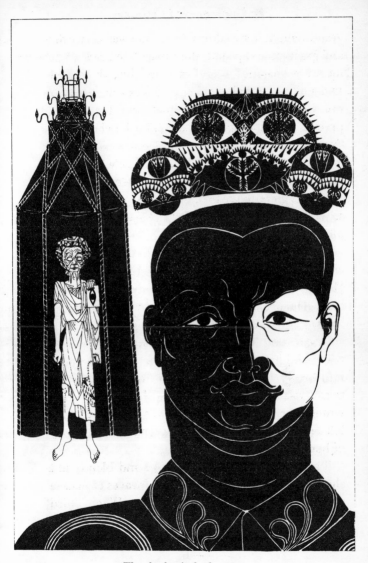

The dealer in body parts

the woman was gone. A soldier, in the uniform of the Neighbours, was leaning over her.

'The Peace of God,' he said. He was of the People, from the country, and with country courtesy he bowed, his hands pressed together as in prayer, at the level of his mouth and chin. That meant the soldier considered Third to be his equal.

She plainly wasn't. Third grunted and sat up. 'Peace of God,' she murmured, and did not bother to bow. She tried to stand up, to regain her place in line. The soldier helped her to her feet, but kept a grip on her arm, and would not let her move back towards the dealer's stall.

'Perhaps you would like something to eat?' he asked, grinning stupidly, with a battery of green, misshapen teeth. He was very ugly, with no chin and a large Adam's apple, and creases across his neck.

'Yes,' said Third, immediately, whatever it was he wanted from her, though she was still feeling queasy. 'In there.' There was a small shop that sold dried insects in glass jars. Some of them were coated in sugar.

'No, no, you cannot eat there,' he said, and pulled her with him.

'But that is what I want,' she protested, looking wistfully back at the window full of insects. What sort of crazy man was this? Did he want a prostitute? She, Third, was no prostitute, he must see

36

that. She was Dastang Tze-See, which meant Desperate Flies in Filth. Desperate Flies filled their wombs, as she did, with other forms of life. No man would go near them. There were silly, nasty stories of men finding Sharks in wait inside them. He had seen her in the line, he must know that. So what did he want?

He took her to a proper food wagon where families ate, with a sign and a man in an apron, and he bought her roast pork and bean shoots and rice, and she nearly fainted again, from the smell, and from wonder.

She crammed her mouth full of it. The skin on the pork had actually been rubbed with salt, and it was crisp and moist with fat, and the bean shoots were hot and fresh and clean tasting, and the rice was hefty and drenched in soy.

'Is it good?' the soldier asked.

Third shrugged with equivocation, her cheeks round and shiny with grease. It was not wise to appear too grateful. The soldier watched her as she ate, still smiling. If only, she thought, he would stop grinning and hide those teeth. Poor people should never smile. She was considering whether she had the strength to run away from him, when he said, 'I have to go now.'

She looked at him, eyes slightly narrowed, still chewing.

'I must return to the barracks. Look, meet me here tomorrow, this time, and we will have another meal.'

'All right,' shrugged Third.

'You will be here? You will not go back to that line?'

Third worked a piece of pork loose from between her teeth. The line was her business.

'I'll give you money, you won't have to.'

'I'll be here,' said Third, scowling.

'Tomorrow, then,' he said, and turned sideways to move through the crowd.

'Hoi!' Third called after him, and he looked around. 'Why are you doing this?'

'For the sake of the People,' he said, no longer smiling, and gave her another equal's bow.

The next day he was there, waiting for her. That made him even more of a mystery. He bought her the food and then began to tell her about himself.

'I am not very good with numbers,' he said, and smiled as if he had made a joke. 'I was not much good at school. But I am good in the army.'

He is not very intelligent, Third decided. That is why he smiles. For some reason, this made her smile too, and feel indulgent.

'Before that,' the soldier said with innocent assurance that she was finding this interesting, or in some way necessary, 'I was a priest.'

In the real days before the war, all young men had been priests instead of soldiers. He must have chosen to become one. Why, wondered Third, is he telling me all this?

'I had the shaved head. The yellow robes. And I did not work, I was given food. When someone died, I sat with them and listened to the story of the one who had died. We sat like this for hours.' He showed her how he sat, hands on their shoulders, rocking. 'I wrote the story down, and put it in the temple so their history would be known.' He smiled again.

'I would put one third of the food I was given into the ghost boxes to feed the dead. Many of the priests did not do this, they kept the food for themselves, but that is wrong. The food is meant for the dead. So they will not feel alone.'

Does he believe it? Does he believe in ghost boxes and life histories? What does he want from me? The answer when it came was so simple that Third felt foolish for not understanding before.

He wants, she understood, a wife. Oh, poor man. That's it, he has been a priest and his time is up – all young men were priests for two years, and then they married, and now is his time to marry. She found his adherence to the pattern touching. It was almost mathematical. And sad. For this man was ugly.

His name was Crow. Crows were omens of death. The family had been given a cursed name as a punishment, and so they were outcasts, except now, when soldiers were needed. As a priest he would have been shunned. Willing and smiling, she saw him, willing and smiling. No one of any station would want a family history written by someone called Crow.

'You have not told me your first name,' she said. Only after she said it, did she realise that it was exactly what she should have said. That was the pattern. You know the last name, and only ask the first name later. When you are courting.

He told her, and she had to close her eyes with embarrassment, shut out the world. Oh, it was not possible, poor, poor, ugly man.

His name, in a certain light, meant Nourisher of the East. It could also mean, more simply, Dung. Crow Dung with the constant smile.

And I am ugly, too, she thought. Oh she knew that, too. She was short and bow-legged, with a thick waist and thick wrists. He wants a wife who is not beautiful, and he wants one of no social standing. He wants a wife to be grateful. And yet ... there was something else. He was a country man. Perhaps he was also kind?

A kind man, however ugly, who wants a wife is an opportunity. Very well, Crow Dung, she thought. I am sick of hunger. I am sick of noise and people's sheets hanging out over my window. But this is being very hard. I also think you have virtues. I will see.

'I am a country girl,' she told him. 'The City confuses me. But I have, I am told, great skills. The thing a woman needs in house work is proportion. That, I have always had. My family used to call me Little Princess, because princesses have time to arrange flowers. I had no time, but I was quick enough to arrange all things. That sounds like I am boasting.'

Third looked down, shyly. She was surprised at how easy it was for her to become a country girl.

'But I love beauty. And I love things to have a place. And I love the space between things.' She found she was telling the truth.

'I often think the stars have a place. When I put the mat and the bowl and the jug of sauce on the floor I think: these also have a place. Like the stars.' And she smiled.

Oh Third, she thought, you are shameless. Crow Dung grinned and grinned.

Right, she thought.

The next morning, her Blood Agent came. 'I have fallen heir to great fortune,' she told him. 'I do not need you.'

'What about my ten per cent?' he asked.

Third saw his ten per cent ever so much more clearly than he did. She threw it over him, her blood, very exactly ten per cent of what she usually gave him. He stumbled backwards, squawking. He knew very well the blood of Dastang Tze-See often had disease, though he still sold it. His bagpipe creature made sucking noises, sensing its feed. It took ten per cent, too.

Well, she thought watching him go, now we will see. I can always get another Blood Agent. But she still had the marks on her arm.

Crow Dung did come courting, with heavy formality. 'I come to visit the young Mademoiselle,' he said, bowing in his army uniform. He was so proud of being in the army. Third thought he looked ridiculous.

He had brought her a gift. 'I saw this,' he said and passed her a gift box made of glazed and woven reed, 'and I thought: someone in my position cannot arrive without something to show for himself.'

Why don't you ask me about the marks on my arm? Third thought. Why don't you ask me how it is that I am alive? She looked at the gift box, and her lip curled, and she passed it back to him. 'I don't want it,' she said.

Third had a beast in the back of her head, and it

was born of hunger and filth; filth and disorder and shame, like a sharp stench. The beast said, I must have this. The beast said, I will not get it, I have never got anything without ripping something out of myself. She confused Crow Dung with people like her Blood Agent. She did not realise that she was hateful to him.

Whenever he visited she insulted him. 'You are common soldier. Some sergeant, you say. I cannot be seen with you. I am of good family. It is wrong. Why do you keep coming here?'

And Crow would keep smiling. Is this some kind of joke to you? she thought.

When he was not there, when she was no longer bitter and anxious and ready to be aggrieved, it came to her that perhaps Crow understood. He understood why she was angry, though she herself did not. Either that, or he was too stupid to notice. I must, she told herself, stop thinking of people as stupid. Who am I, Dastang Tze-See, to call anyone stupid?

She ate her meals alone. She ate a kind of curd that was made from sewage, processed by micro-organisms. It was called War Tofu, and was odourless and absolutely tasteless.

She was cold at night, shivering like a dog having dreams, under a single thin blanket.

Oh, Lord Buddha, send him back, and I will beg

43

his forgiveness, she would say, to the night sky that
had no stars.

And he would come back, and she would rail at
him, and Crow would smile and bow. She was
behaving exactly as a country girl should.

Then he asked her to the Ceremony.

This was so unasked for, so wonderful, that
Third could not help but throw him out in a fury.
Ceremony? How could she go with him, Crow
Dung, to the Ceremony? She was already asked,
she had many friends, he was to go away and
silently ask himself where he thought he was.

It was so beyond hope that anyone would take her
to the Ceremony.

The People had a Prince. The mention of his
name was enough to make the bottom edge of their
eyes sting with salt tears, for the Prince was from
the old days, when the Country was Unconquered.
He was fat and healthy, with fine white teeth, and
he was kind and clever. Even the Neighbours could
see his fine qualities. That was why, thought Third,
they put him back on the throne. Under their noses,
he prayed for the deliverance of his People. Third
kept pictures of him from the papers on her walls.
She prayed to him. She loved him, not in the way
you love a man, but in the way you love yourself and
the things that make you. She was fierce on the
subject of the Prince.

And Crow had asked her to the Ceremony, where she would see him.

She thought she was not worthy. She thought she was ugly and dark-skinned and could not dress suitably. When Crow asked her, she wanted to hide, hide her head and run from the house.

'I am going with someone else,' she told him. She was so poor her nervous hands had nothing to play with.

'That someone is very honoured,' replied Crow.

I hate you, thought Third. Why are you so honeyed? You are like a wind-up doll.

'I am, I hope, a friend,' continued Crow. 'So, please, I hope you will find this to your taste and that you will wear it to the Ceremony with your friends.'

He laid out on the floor of Third's house – oh, in the old days, she would not have had a house by herself, and if she did, he could not have been there alone with her, it was all a shadow show, but he wanted to believe. It was he who wanted to believe. He laid out on the floor a new dress. It was black, deep black, fine black, not the sort of black that goes patchy when it rains, good black. And it had gold leaves on it. Third almost wept.

'Why did you do that? I did not ask you to do that!' she raged. 'I don't need your dresses.'

'Of course. Oh, that is evident,' replied Crow.

'But it would be such an honour for me if you wore it.'

Third felt like weeping on her knees. 'I will consider,' she said. She had two dresses that had long ago forgotten what colour they were. When Crow was gone, she held the dress up to the light. The light caught on the leaves. There were twenty-one of them. An auspicious number. The dress-maker knew and probably wondered if anyone else knew or cared that the dress was an oracle. I care, Third said to the silent dressmaker. Then she felt panic. How will I tell him that I will go with him? I have been so rude. I have sent him away, will he come back?

He did, but with no gifts. That is good, Third thought, you have given me enough. No gifts. It is time I treated you with some respect.

And so she bowed when he entered. 'Mr Crow,' she said. 'We find ourselves in strange situations, with no guide. And I think: here is one of the People, who serves in the army because he thinks this is right. Now this is an honourable thing. And I should not despise his rank. Or fear it. And I think: my fabled friends are as nothing to this one man who cares so much for his People and for his work. I should not be hard. And so I make an easy decision. One that is happy for me. I tell my friends: there is a special person who must take priority at this time.

Next year this might not be the case. Perhaps I will not have the opportunity next year. Life is such that we are only given the opportunity to do the right thing once. And it is our duty to do the right thing.'

And so she went to the Ceremony.

The Ceremony was in the Old City, with its streets of stone. A foreign city, she thought as she walked through it. She hated right angles. So many of the broad avenues met at right angles, and she knew that foreigners must have made them. But suddenly the streets went small and sheltering again, and she thought: we built in stone once too. So she did not hate the stone any longer. She and Crow walked to the central square.

The square was the most ancient part of the city of Saprang Song. There were umbrella pine all around it, and temples. The temples were made of volcanic rock or brick, with thin and delicate spires and smiling stone faces that were images of the Buddha. In the middle of the square was a con- course of green, tended grass with a gravel track around it, and bleachers along one side. It was used mainly for horse races now. Once a year, it was used for the Ceremony . . .

A temporary stage had been built in the centre of the green. A small orchestra in formal evening wear sat on it, miserable with the heat. Rows and rows of priests, in yellow, with freshly shaven heads, sat in

The Ceremony

pride of place, just in front of the stage. Behind them, on the grass or in the bleachers, were the prosperous people of the city. They sat on blankets with picnic hampers, and they wore the clothes of the Big Country. They had beautiful children, little girls in pink or orange trousers with white socks and shiny black shoes, who ran laughing, holding ice creams. The women sat serenely on rugs, like princesses, their legs folded under them, their hair in smooth, oiled domes with shiny tin stars in them.

Third only had one shirt, which she had to wear with her new dress. The shirt was cheap cotton, with faded blue flowers, frayed around the collar. Her dull, unoiled hair, pulled back severely and tied with a bit of coloured yarn, was that of a peasant. She clutched her meagre little beaded purse and walked without looking around her, blind with shame.

'Sergeant! Sergeant!' a voice was calling. 'Sergeant Crow!' A man, sitting on a folding chair, wearing sunglasses and a uniform and a black beret, was waving to them. He was smoking a cigarette in a holder made of bone, his teeth clenched about it as he called again. He wore polished boots to the knee.

As they approached, Crow bowed, grinning, and bowed again, hands held high above his head. 'Colonel! Sir! Colonel! Sir!' Crow said in an unpleasant, barking, official kind of voice. The

49

Colonel's wife, with an unperturbed smile, looked at, then away from, and finally through Third and Crow. She smoothed down her trouser suit, and adjusted her sunglasses.

'We find this Ceremony most important for the People,' the Colonel granted. 'A sense of continuity is most important, don't you feel, Sergeant. Under the circumstances.' The Colonel had a long flexible leather cane, which he kept slapping idly against his boot.

'Certainly, Sir. The wisdom is apparent,' Crow said, briskly. Even in his new green coolsuit and slicked black hair he looked wretched and small, dipping and bowing. Third moved from one foot to the other. The Colonel's wife tapped her knees with the tips of her fingers. A pair of earplugs were whispering music to her. On top of the hamper was a bar of broken-open chocolate. In a moment, politeness would demand that the Colonel ask Crow to watch the Ceremony with them.

Then Crow said, 'I must make excuses, Colonel, Sir. But we have seats in the bleachers, and we must make our way to them.'

'Of course, of course,' said the Colonel, already looking elsewhere. He gave a lax wave of dismissal with his hand as it hung over the arm of the chair.

'It has been delightful, Sir. Delightful, Madame,' Crow assured them.

As Third walked away, she heard the wife say, her voice too loud because of her earplugs, 'Hmm! The Crow and his Turtle.'

Third stormed up the steps of the bleachers ahead of Crow. She pushed her way past a seller of sparrows in cages, and trod on the toes of people who stood up to let her pass. If I am a peasant, I will act like a peasant, she thought. She sat down without smiling and greeting the people next to her, without looking at Crow when he joined her. She answered him with fierce, short grunts.

'Look, Third, people from the Big Country,' he whispered. Third had never seen Big People before. They had been given special places under a canopy by the stage. They arrived all together, lumbering like houses, tall, clumsy, with enormous booted feet, and they did indeed have skin the colour of plucked chickens. Their wives, towering columns of crumpled cotton, dropped down on to their deck chairs, relieved of their own weight. They were all so large, it seemed, swollen with power, sprawling on the chairs, chewing gum. They frightened Third, and made her angry. What are they doing if they don't want to be here, she thought. We don't want them. They don't understand. They don't believe. This is our country. One of them had orange hair and was covered in speckles, like a fish. Or a Shark.

Suddenly there was a sound like the sea, and all the People stood up and roared. It must be the Prince. Third looked wildly around her and finally saw, in the air, coming out of the north, a van, held aloft by four giant swans, and there was a man in it, and Third felt something unexpected catch in her chest. Yes, yes it was him, and he looked just like her pictures. He smiled and waved, and flung up both his arms over his head, like the Spirit of Happiness. The van swept low over the crowd, and he threw out handfuls of white lotus blossom. His suit and his tie were white. The swans were white, their long necks held straight out, their wings whistling. They began to pump backwards, furiously, and the carriage was lowered towards the stage. Guards ran out to steady it. The orchestra struck up a cheerful, see-sawing song that the Prince had composed himself. Before the van was quite down, he launched himself over the side, like a fat, happy schoolboy. 'Up! Up!' he shouted, and suddenly, from behind the stage, a flock of balloons was released.

They were silver, thousands of them, one for each year of the Country's history. They all seemed to be blown towards the bleachers. They wriggled their way through the air, towards the People, and each of them, in silver, was a sculptured portrait of the Prince, and each one of them said, with the

Prince's voice, 'An offering. An offering to the Buddha. A holy offering.' At the ends of each of their tethers, which were segmented metal bands, was a three-fingered hand. The hands reached out, and the People eagerly surged forward, reaching over each other's shoulders to place earrings or rice cakes into them. Third reached out with one small brass coin. The balloon's hand felt warm and rubbery. 'Thank you, sister,' the balloon said. Third's face was reflected back at her from the Prince's own.

'To Heaven! To Heaven!' beamed the Prince, and the balloons sucked in air, and swelled, and slowly, en masse, began to rise. The Prince urged them on with great windmill circlings of his arms. The priests, who had been still, leapt to their feet and began to bash gongs and bells and cymbals. The balloons interwove with each other, flashing with reflected sunlight against the pure blue of the sky. Spots of sunlight flittered across the crowd, dazzling them, making them yelp. Then rising above all the other noise, slow and heavy, there began a song.

It was an old song, one Third could almost remember, one she thought everyone had forgotten. The woman next to her reached across and took her left hand. All the People linked hands, as if they were flowers at feast. Crow took her hand too. Oh,

53

she thought, we are not defeated, we are not broken. We are still the Unconquered People. A beautiful young girl of the People ran on to the stage, her face crumpled with the effort of not laughing, and kissed the Prince, and the People cheered. Many good things are real, thought Third. I am going to have a husband. I am going to have a life. The balloons dwindled until they looked like a host of daytime stars. They would rise so high, and then rupture, but their souls would go on.

The Prince looked up and waved. 'Bye bye,' he called to them, like a child. Crow, faithful with his broken smile, was looking steadily at Third.

Three months later, the wars began again.

PART THREE

A Bird, Singing

THE BIG MEN changed their minds. Who could say why the Big People did things? They gave weapons to the rebels this time, who were still in the hills like an unhealed sore. These weapons could do something new. Blowing Kisses, it was called.

A nurse led Third through the corridors of the hospital. The way the sounds and whispering reverberated made Third feel ill. Lined up on pallets all along the halls were the new wounded, muttering, often to themselves. They looked very calm, without a mark, except for strange bruises, as if someone had brushed them with ash.

Crow was on a bed, in a ward. There was nothing wrong with him that Third could see, except for a patch of skin on his forehead like the skin of a rotten apple. Wanly, he smiled when he saw her, and held out his hand. It was a monk's hand, with slender, flute-playing fingers. Third looked about her in dazed confusion. The nurse had to help her step over people to get to his bed.

'They *found* you,' murmured Crow.

'A lady came and told me you were here, and led me.'

'Blessed lady.' His hand still reached out for her, but she did not approach.

'What is wrong with you?' Third demanded. She could see no wounds.

'There is a hot little egg in the middle of my head, and it is hatching. I can hardly see you. Come closer. Sit on the bed.'

Third, who had hardly known what to do or say before, was now overwhelmed with mortification. There were people about them everywhere. It was bad enough having to talk in front of them. Nevertheless, she jumped up on to the very foot of the bed, her legs dangling so far from the floor. She coughed to clear her throat, and began to talk of innocent things. 'I saw your aunt as you asked me. She is very well. She gave me tea. She has bought herself a dog. One of those small nasty ones with a face like a Chinese dragon. Stupid thing, to have a dog, you have to feed it.'

'I hope you will be friends,' said Crow.

'She treated me well enough,' Third said, with a shrug. 'My wedding coat is nearly finished.' She had become a seamstress, working in the night, and she was saving scraps of cloth for it. 'It is all white. It has a white dove on it, and it has a white portrait of the Prince.'

Crow settled back and let his hand fall. 'Tell me about it,' he asked.

'That is all there is to tell, just that,' she replied, embarrassed.

'It has a high, white starched collar and the winged shoulders,' he said. His eyes were dim and loving, looking through all the hospital, at the coat, seeing it clearly, or perhaps another coat that he remembered.

'Yes, that's it,' said Third in a thin voice, though it wasn't.

'That is good. That is a very country coat. But you must not let anyone see it. Not with the Prince's portrait on it. The rebels hate him. They will hate you. Promise me you will hide the coat.'

Third was not pleased. Hide her coat. What was he talking about? 'The rebels are People too.'

'They have changed. When they ask, do not say you almost married a soldier. When they ask, say you married a fighter for the People, and that the foreigners killed him. It will be true.'

'What nonsense!' said Third. 'What is wrong with you? I can see nothing wrong with you.' She looked about her at the other wounded. There seemed to be nothing wrong with any of them. 'When will you be out of that bed?'

'Soon,' said Crow.

'There!' said Third. Her legs ached from hanging over the floor. Angrily, she moved further on to the bed.

59

When she looked back, Crow was holding his hand over his head, watching his fingers wave, like wind chimes in a light breeze. He began to talk even worse nonsense.

'Hearts go up like balloons,' he said. 'Hearts ring like voices, echo like clouds. Cobbles underfoot. Always stumble. Drains. When looking upward. There is a bird singing.'

'What are you saying?' Third whispered, looking around her. She wriggled further up the bed and finally took his hand. He grabbed it fiercely.

'There is a *bird singing*,' he insisted, his face shuddering as he began to cry. 'They are pulling off its legs and wings, but it is still singing.'

'Ssssh! There is no bird.'

'There is! But no one can see it!'

'It is this place,' said Third, miserably. 'All this noise. It is confusing.' Badly frightened now, she squeezed his hand, and covered it with her other hand.

'When I was a boy,' he began. 'Strange cities. Always there. Always there. Never left me.'

Was he trying to tell a story? You had to listen when someone finally spoke. Third peered at him anxiously. He stared ahead, as if moving at high speed. Then he began to chant.

It was a priestly mantra. The words meant nothing, they were deliberate nonsense. Meaning would distract. 'I ing a na. I ing a na. I ing a na,' over and over very softly.

'That's better. That's better,' Third told him. His voice faded away altogether, and he went very still, his wet eyes still on her.

She had never realised before that he was beautiful. She had never seen his body. His legs were hot under the white sheet, and his chest was bare down to the waist, smooth and brown and surprisingly fleshy. His lips were only slightly parted over his crowded, crooked mouth, and a tear still crept down his face. She looked at his hand, and played with his long supple fingers. Even the hand looked more substantial now, veined and broad and masculine.

She coughed to clear her throat. 'I have been thinking,' she said. 'This city is no good for us. It is a bad place, with all these Desperate Flies crowding in because of the war. We could go back to my village. There is much orderly planting there. It is in the west, away from where the war is now. There is a lot of land there, because all the men have been killed. We could get married there. All the girls will be in a chain of flowers. They will sing the song of the true knight who climbed the mountain. They will steam fish with ginger.' It seemed to her that Crow nodded, slightly, yes.

'We could look for my old house,' she said. 'They

don't die, the old houses, they are iike oaks. I'm
sure it will know me. It is stupid to keep a dog when
you can have a house. A house is shelter.' For some
reason she felt tears suddenly sting her eyes. That
was foolish. 'Ah, well,' she sighed, and let go of his
hand, patting it. She pulled around her work bag,
and took out her quilting. 'We can talk about it
later. I will stay here.'

A lady came towards her, in a white white, big
breasted, in the squeaking white shoes of the Big
People, and suddenly she looked to Third like one
of the other White Ladies, a giant hen.

'You had better go now,' the hen said, warily.

Third could not help but grin. She had to cover
her mouth.

The woman looked very displeased, perhaps
insulted, and she strode, still squeaking, briskly
round the side of the bed, and felt Crow's forehead.
Crow, who had been smiling at her with Third,
seemed to freeze with embarrassment at being
touched by another woman in her presence.

'I will do that for him,' said Third, shyly. She
lifted up his hand, which was still warm, to pull the
sheet up under it, to hide Crow's body from this
woman. Abruptly the woman snatched the hand
from her, and held it by the wrist.

Then she leaned over, so that Third had to look
at her terrible face with its strained smile. 'There

The death of Crow

is no point to you staying any longer,' she said.

'Tuh,' said Third, and made a gesture of throwing the hen a bit of slug.

'It is best that you go now, really,' said the woman, who was actually shaking from fatigue. 'Come along now.' She tried to take Third's elbow to ease her down from the bed. Third pulled it away.

'We are talking about family business,' said Third, haughtily. 'We do not want to be interrupted.'

The hen put a hand on her own forehead, and closed her eyes for a moment. She sighed and said, 'He will be doing no more talking.'

'Then let him sleep,' said Third and picked up her quilting. 'I will stay here.'

'He is dead,' said the woman. 'I'm sorry. We need the bed.'

'Don't be silly,' said Third. 'He was talking to me a moment ago. Go away and leave us alone.' She turned away from the woman, and took up her needle and thread.

'All right,' said the woman, wearily. 'You can have a few more minutes.' Third heard her squeaking away.

She turned to Crow, who seemed to nod his head in approval. The tear on his face still moved. It touched the pillow and was gone, absorbed. Suddenly, even though it was daylight with people all around them, Third laid her head on his bosom. 'I am like the cat, sometimes,' she told him. 'When things are near me, I pretend I do not want them. I think I do not care for them, in case they are taken away. Most things get taken away. It is like that when people are hurt. When they are near, I give them no sympathy, in case they take advantage. It is only when I leave the room, that I can weep for them. Do you understand?' It seemed to her that he did. His chest was very still. She sat up, and moved the sheet a little higher. 'Tell me about when you were a boy,' she asked him, patting the fold of the sheet. He didn't answer. She sat and thought nothing, only nothing, for a very long time.

Until the hen came squeaking back. 'This time you must go. This is really too bad. There are people on the floor!' Third looked at her, unblinking. The woman suddenly shouted. 'There are sick people. You must leave!' Third would not move. 'My dear woman, I know this is terrible, but there are others. Please go. Please.' The woman looked around her helplessly, and then left.

Third stared at the body. It was very still, like statues of the reclining Buddha, but it was going ugly again. The teeth were sticking out further from the mouth, and the eyes, under heavy lids, were dry and crossed. A fly picked its way across

the lips. Third, distracted, waved it away. It came back.

There was a bustle behind her, and the woman was coming with a man now, a doctor, and she was abject and pleading and servile, saying that she had asked, that she had tried everything. The doctor, aged and respectable, sat on the bed next to Third. He expressed his condolences and said that he did not know why it was that fine young men had to die, except that it could not possibly be the will of God. Could she see, though, that the bed was needed for other people's loved ones? Would she go? 'Up, up my daughter,' he said, trying to coax her.

Third suddenly snarled, and tried to hit him with her dogged little fist. He ducked and it missed. 'First Sister was withered by Sharks! Second Sister ...' she yelled, and choked and tried to hit him again. Her second sister sat in an airport window for the Big People, and arranged her hair so that the sores would not show. Her mother had starved herself to death so that they would have enough to eat. 'Go away! Go away and leave us alone!' The doctor leapt down from the bed, slipping on his leather soles. Third flung her quilting after him as he scuttled away, and she sat and wept, not knowing why she was weeping, and hid her face.

Suddenly it was dark. There was soft moaning, and

the clatter of instruments on moving trolleys, and the sound of flies. All that Third thought was that it was late, time for her to go. She jumped down from the bed, walked down the passageway between the beds, and nodded politely to a nurse as she passed. Somehow she found her way down the stairs and through the hallways, to the large, heavy main glass doors. It was not until she saw them, swinging, saw her own reflected image like a ghost in the blackness beyond, that she realised, or else remembered, that Crow was dead.

She gave a little yelp, and covered her mouth, and turned and ran. She had not looked at him properly, knowing he was dead, to remember his face. She had not asked the nurse what would happen next, what the funeral arrangements would be. In a panic, she ran down the corridors, which all looked the same, which all echoed, which all were crowded with dying men who looked the same. 'Crow! Crow!' she called for him, though it was stupid, he couldn't answer. She ran up steps, she remembered steps, to the room she thought he would be in, but all she found there was an empty bed among the full ones. She ran to another ward. 'Oh no. How stupid. Oh no,' she said to herself in a breathless voice. In that room all the beds were full of different people. Wrong room, back again to the first one. But all the beds in that room too, all of them, were full. Right room, wrong room. She saw a nurse, one she didn't recognise, and grabbed her arm.

'Many pardons. Many pardons. Can you tell me where my husband, Crow, Nourisher of the East, is?'

The nurse, tired beyond endurance, simply shook her head and pointed towards a doctor in the shadows.

'Doctor,' said Third, 'Doctor, my husband is dead. He died here, and now I can't find his body, and I have to make arrangements!'

The doctor, one she didn't recognise, took her arm. 'You are the next of kin?'

'Yes, yes,' she said, trembling like a bird.

'Then don't worry. Go home and try to sleep. We will contact you about the arrangements later. Come now, this way. I will show you the way out.'

'Thank you, Sir. Many pardons,' said Third and looked back over her shoulder, hoping by accident to catch one last glimpse of Crow.

The main doors swung again, and this time Third seemed to catch the reflection of many ghosts. They crowded the main hall. The doctor nodded to her and light flashed on his spectacles. Light danced on the doorway as it settled shut: Third was outside on the hospital steps, and the sky overhead was full of light and a crackling sound.

Fireworks. Why, thought Third, why are there fireworks?

'Oh, Crow,' she whispered, as the sky was spangled. 'How could you leave me? What do I do now?' Green and red opened up in the sky, flower-bursts of light, loose and shimmering. She had never known him as a man. That was what it was for, finally, the wary approach, the angry rebuff, the gradual drawing together. It was meant to end with her lying next to that beautiful body. That was what she wanted.

She realised then that she loved him. For his beautiful body, for his broken face, and for his heart, what was inside him. Oh Third, fool, it is too late to realise that. What good is that now? Like the cat.

It was not enough. Was it all for nothing? Third watched the fireworks.

Then she understood life histories. Why people told them. They wanted to save something. Suddenly, as badly as she had ever needed anything, Third needed a priest. She saw the spires of a temple, dark against ochre sky. She ran.

Across the hospital square, past a fountain, as if the fireworks were bombs, and she were dodging them. She ran up the temple steps to the great carved doors. They flickered in the pink-white fireworks light.

69

The closed temples

They were locked. Third tried to shake them, and felt the heavy bolts behind them. 'Peace of God? Peace of God?' she called, panting, in a weak voice.

When had temple doors ever been barred? Suddenly angry, she slammed her fist against them, pounding, and heard how small the noise was in the rolling darkness behind them.

'It's closed,' a voice said behind her. An old man was squatting on the steps, hunched over a bowl of rice, twisting round on his haunches to look at her. Third stared at him.

'The temple is closed,' he repeated.

'Are you a priest?' Third demanded, avid.

'What? No, oh no. All the priests have fled. Haven't you heard? They refused to join the army, and the Neighbours started putting them in jail. Where have you been hiding?'

'Where did they go?'

The old man laughed. 'Ho! Even if I knew, I wouldn't tell. One of them set himself alight in the main square. Where they have the Ceremony. You must know that. The Neighbours will not let anyone bring flowers to that place. They will not let anyone mourn.'

'There must be priests somewhere. Have they all gone, all the temples?'

'Ah,' the old man shrugged. 'Who can say?'

71

Third ran from temple to temple, all across the city, and they were all closed. The fireworks erupted overhead. Victory, the Neighbours were claiming, in only two months' time. The summer streets were full of laughing people. A parade of street players jostled past Third. They carried huge lights that blazed into her face. Their aloof painted faces smiled as rockets whined overhead. An old woman picking over fruit glanced at Third, blinking with heavy-lidded, reptilian eyes. No one knew who Crow was, no one knew he was dead, no one knew of the grief that Third carried within her, like a pouch of pus. 'Have you seen a priest?' she asked, and people passed, pretending not to hear. There were soldiers, celebrating, waving their weapons in the air. You will die, Third thought, coldly.

It grew late. Third saw a man bowed under a machine, carrying it on his back, delivering it. He wore scraps of cloth that had been sewn together to look like an important person's suit of clothes. The fireworks stopped, the streets began to clear. A line of students meandered arm in arm towards Third. They wore white T-shirts splattered with rebel slogans in red paint. They wound themselves, laughing, around a fire hydrant.

'Forget your priests,' they told Third. 'The priests can't help you, they just sit on their yellow backsides.' They burbled a mocking imitation of a

The Coca-Cola girl

holy chant. 'Pieces of God. Pieces of God. Pieces of money.' They wheeled drunkenly away, like a straggly white worm.

Very suddenly, Third was alone in the middle of the wide avenue. She heard the sound of wind move across the cobbles. She knew, with the sensation of claws sinking into her back, that she would not be able to mourn. There was no way left for her to mourn. It had been taken away. She looked up at the sky. How nice it would be, she thought, to be a balloon and simply drift away, to somewhere else.

'Hi!' piped a shrill little voice. It was an advertisement, standing suddenly in front of her. 'I'm the Coca-Cola girl!' It thrust a glass of fizzing soft drink up towards her.

'No thank you. Go away,' said Third.

Advertisements came alive at night, and were allowed to climb down from their signs. They were slightly flattened, like cartoon figures, with sharp creases along the edges of the arms and legs and heads. This one was a little girl, with pigtails, and wide Mickey Mouse eyes, and a red gingham dress, and three-fingered hands. She broke into a song.

> Coca-Cola gives you life
> Gives you hope
> Gives you strength
> To carry through the day!

Third turned and walked quickly away from her. The advertisement was programmed to sing, to someone, and there was no one else. She followed Third down the steep slope of the avenue, skipping. Her shiny black shoes went pop-pop-pop on the cobbles because they were suction cups. Third covered her ears, and began to run. The advertisement ran with her, dancing. 'Busy people like you like Coke because it gives them instant energy to face the brisk life of the city,' the advertisement pleaded, wishing perhaps it was able to say something else. 'One glass of Coke gives you all major vitamins and minerals, including the B and C groups so necessary to cope with stress. Stay healthy! Stay happy! Drink Coke!'

'Go away!' shouted Third.

The advertisement staggered back a step. Then she began to sing again. '. . . gives you life/Gives you hope/Gives you strength . . .'

Give me my husband, thought Third. There was scaffolding, unassembled, beside a building. Third picked up a length of pipe and spun round and smashed the advertisement as hard as she could.

She hit it on the shoulder. The arm broke off. It was full of red, rather dry meat, and did not bleed. Third squawked in horror at how easily it broke apart. The thing kept on singing '. . . gives you life . . .' Third hit it again and again, to make it quiet, to

75

stop it singing, to knock it away from her. Its skirt
slipped off and the naked little legs kept on dancing
with nothing above them. The slightly flattened
head lay on the ground, its cheeks still the colour of
peaches, and it was still singing. Third kicked it,
and it spun around and around like a plate, skitter-
ing down the hill. Third could hear the sound of the
wind again, hollow. She drew in shaky breaths,
feeling ill, and finally wanted to go home.

She had to walk back across the Old City, and
through the heaps. She knew each heap by name –
the Scarecrow, or the Fist Raised Towards Heaven.
It was the time of the dogs. They barked, wild and
unchecked, as she climbed up and over the roofs of
other people's houses, towards her own. Once she
was inside it, it turned its light on, and there it was,
bare and grey and streaked and smelling of fungus.
She groaned and fell face down on the bed.

She heard the sound of many children playing
and a band playing the Prince's song. Oh, she
thought gratefully, oh, I'm falling asleep. As soon
as she thought that, she was wide awake, with the
iron knowledge that Crow was dead. Crow, she
thought, I'm sorry I cannot mourn. It must be a
terrible thing to lie unmourned. You must wander
unsatisfied. She lay unmoving for a very long time,
eyes open. Perhaps this is what it is like to be dead,

she thought. Outside a cat was mewling, caught in a trap. People ate them now. Then Third remembered. There was one thing Crow had asked her to do.

She lit a candle and took out her wedding coat. It was lumpy, misshapen, made of scraps, unfinished. She saw that now. Everything in her life had been like that. She knelt and cut open the floor of her room, and the house shivered in pain, and she lifted up the lip of flesh. The hollow in the floor began, immediately, to seep moisture. She wrapped the coat in a plastic garbage bag, so that it would not be stained, and she laid it in the hole, smoothing it down so that it would not wrinkle. She managed to squeeze a tear out of herself, like liquor from an unripe wound, and she closed the flesh over the coat, and covered that with matting. It would heal shut.

Then Third stood up and walked, dazed, out of her house, she did not know where. Direction chose her.

She found herself at the edge of the main temple square. The umbrella pine rose and fell like waves around her. The bleachers were there, for the horse races, but where the stage had been, there were only blowing bits of paper and a patch of white ash. Lights bobbed idly about it. It was guarded. Third was turning to go, when she heard, within the wind, the sound of a cry.

77

The cry was small and plaintive and sweet. It sounded like Third felt, as if something had been lost. It was coming from under the trees nearby, a whistling that rose up at the end, like a question, like no other noise Third had heard before. She ducked under the branches. There was something on the ground, a bundle, and the light caught it. It was a bird that was making the noise, its feathers puffed out in the wind, a young bird. She knelt beside it, her throat clenching like a fist. The bird was a crow.

'Crow!' she said and picked it up and finally, gently, softly, the tears came, in an easy film down her face. She rocked with it, back and forth. 'Crow. Crow. Crow.'

Suddenly the lights were harsh in her eyes, and she turned away.

'What are you doing here?' demanded one voice.

'Why are you crying?' demanded another.

They were Neighbours. Third could only see their shadows behind the lights.

'I am crying because of this bird. It has been blown from its nest. It is so small.'

'You are not supposed to be here. Get out.'

Third stood up, and bowed to them, and ran. She held the bird to her face and breathed on it. A crow was an omen of death, but a crow that sings

A Bird, Singing

was something more. There is a bird singing. He had said that.

Weeping, consoled, Third was sure that Nourisher of the East had found his way back to her.

PART FOUR

The Crow that Warbled

THE CROW that Warbled grew into a great, ragged-feathered beast, with grey-green scaly legs and claws, and a beak that seemed too large and heavy for its head. It was too big to be kept in a cage; there were perches in all the corners of the room, and linen cloths under its feed tray and a sand box. In one corner of the room was a shrine, with paper flowers that Third had made from chewing-gum wrappers. In frames made of twisted wire were drawings she had made of the Dead: her mother who had starved, her first sister who was withered; her second sister who had sat dead and undiscovered for half a day in an airport window. There was a drawing, too, of Nourisher of the East, looking as plump and healthy as the Prince.

Third had never been told where the funeral was. She was not, after all, the next of kin. She did not know where Nourisher of the East had been cremated, or where the ashes were. When she visited his aunt, the people in the next house smiled and said she was not at home. The fifth time she came they said, still smiling, 'In all fairness, we ought to tell you that, for you, she will never be at home.'

'Tell her,' Third replied. 'That all she has is ashes. I have the soul.'

She had the Crow that Warbled. She called it husband. She bathed it regularly in the cleanest water she could find, and dried it in white cloths, laughing and teasing, and it would tilt its head, as if wondering if she were mad, and that would make her laugh more.

She set it free, over the heaps, from her high window. The Crow that Warbled would hover, high, in the same place for ten or fifteen minutes at a time, and it would sing, and the songs it sang were the songs of the People. Third knew it was a spirit then. How else would it know to sing the morning song at dawn, or the feast songs, or the songs for the Dead? The poor people, in their dangerously shifting heaps of housing, all looked up towards it. They understood the miracle. The wild children who lived like animals in packs under bridges, crept out of the shadows to listen. Old women would hum along with the songs, rocking on slippery mushroom steps, remembering. When the Crow was tired, it would flutter down amongst them and look pointedly at the rice in their bowls. They would chuckle and give Crow some, for they knew it was a ghost, and it was utmost politeness to feed a ghost. They would duck and bow at its arrival, their clasped hands high over their heads in respect. But the Crow always returned to Third. The People would look up at her window then, and wave. She was mistress of the miracle. And Third, for the first time, smiled back.

It was strangers who didn't like the Crow, people who wore the clothes of the Big Country and carried lacquered canes, people who were lost and panicked in the heaps. The Crow would drop on them to say hello, for it thought it was human. It would come singing the song of hospitality, a black Crow, bringer of Death. The strangers would scuttle away, quietly, pursued, holding on to their hats, afraid to run or shout, because that would mean they thought they would die if the Crow touched them, and City People were not supposed to be superstitious. They believed, none the less, and would try to swipe at Crow with their canes. The people of the heaps would point at them and laugh. They would follow in a crowd to see the end of the comedy. The strangers would think they were being chased by the poor. Their faces said that all their most anxious fantasies seemed to be coming true.

People started coming to Third for cures. She found that by laying hands on them, she could send them away at least thinking they were better. She began to grow herbs in window boxes for remedies. People gave her messages for dead relatives, for the

Crow to carry. They bowed to her, hands high over their heads, and called her Widow.

Third had to wear spectacles now. A doctor at the hospital, to which she kept returning, got her a job at his brother's factory. She peered down a microscope, watching crystals grow. The work ruined her eyes.

The crystals were sliced continually as they grew, and Third had to make sure that the pattern on each slice was the same, like rock candy. She found it difficult to keep count of how many she inspected. The machine presented them in groups of ten, and all she had to do was remember how many groups. This confused her.

'I never learned my figures,' she said, smiling behind pebble spectacles. 'I am very ignorant.' There was no shame in admitting this to an educated man.

'Just make a mark with this pencil, one for each group,' said her supervisor, who blamed the war.

She kept track of her change in the market by remembering the colour of the coin. Then the money was devalued, and everyone began to use paper. So she began to remember the faces on the paper instead. She couldn't read the names of the faces, so she gave them the names of people in her old village, and kept their titles. One was landowner, one was doctor, one kept the seed grain.

That way, she had a rough idea of what she was owed.

Then they changed it all around by saying that the value of each note was now what it would be if it had an extra zero on the end of its number. They could not afford to reprint their money.

The day this happened, Third stood weeping in the market, shaking the one note in change she had received from a market dealer. When he looked worn, bored, anything other than guilty or caught out, she became hysterical. She was not even shouting words, just tones of anger. All her money for the week was gone. An older gentleman took her arm, and whispered to her, calmly, trying to make her understand that the money was worth more now. Many people gathered around, to try to explain. They could not all be thieves. Third was mollified in the end. She left with her one note.

But she did not understand. She felt betrayed, as if nothing would ever make sense again. She went home and asked the Crow. The Crow was silent, but it seemed to be a significant silence. The answer was not here, he seemed to say. It lay elsewhere. Everything that made sense was going elsewhere.

So she lived. In the evenings, she sewed, jabbing her fingers with the needle because she couldn't see. The Crow perched beside her, and seemed to watch with interest.

She collected old advertisements. Her babies, she called them. Some of them might have been. They were old, about to die. She hung them on the wall, faded green, rusty red. When she fell asleep, over her sewing, on the floor, they came alive. Their skin was peeling off, and they could no longer sing except in worn, whispering voices. The Crow would try to teach them new songs, but they shook their heads. That was beyond them. They danced around Third as she slept, in the moonlit room, like dreams. In the morning, they would be back on their signs, frozen still and silent.

Third even began to get to know her house. It had not been imprinted to care about who lived in it, but Third dusted its corners, and swept away its old itchy skin, and talked to it until it came to know her and the rhythm of her tread. She knew when it slept, and sat still herself then, to let it rest. Friends told her that it grew fretful and sighed when she was not there, in the market, at work.

There was always work, at the factory, in the heaps, at her quilting: work as the pot bubbled on the stove in the home Third would have made for her husband, work, until, after only two or three years, she became stolid and drab, her skin toughened somehow and polished-looking like old leather. People called her Old Woman. She elbowed her way through the stalls, singing the old songs in a loud shrill voice, pulling a squeaking wooden wagon behind her, a small bow-legged woman in spectacles and a very faded cotton shirt. She counted faces instead of numbers. Everywhere she went, she expounded the miracle of the Crow that Warbled.

'He goes back to the Land of the Dead, to where everything is as it should be, as it was, where the People are still Unconquered,' she said.

The People of Saprang Song could hear the war, its dull roar, its high-pitched hum, but the battles never seemed to reach the Divine Lotus, as if the city were charmed. Over it, over the heaps and the People in them, the Crow that Warbled hovered, singing the old songs.

PART FIVE

No Harm Can Come

THE REBELS won. The news was spread by the packs of ragged orphans who lived wild. They ran through the heaps, and were for once admitted without qualm into the rooms of the People. Outside Saprang Song, in the burnt paddies, the army of the Neighbours and their servants had been destroyed.

The City People celebrated. They built bonfires in the squares and in the narrow passageways between the heaps. They banged on pans to make something like music, and blew through paper on combs. The rebels were the People, like themselves; the People had won. They hung their white sheets out of their windows as a sign of victory. They gathered under Third's window and called for the Crow that Warbled. It hopped excitedly among them, from shoulder to shoulder. They bowed to it, laughing with toothless mouths. They sang with it. They grew drunken and bold, heaping up the banners of the Neighbours on the fire, wrapping themselves in white to jump over the flames. 'Unconquered. Unconquered. Unconquered,' they chanted, hopping up and down in unison. This was not an old song, or an old dance.

93

The night before the rebels came

Third didn't like it. She slipped away unnoticed to her bed.

Almost everyone was asleep, sleeping late, when the rebels came.

Third awoke to the sound of things falling. She heard laughter, loud. She got up, and stumbled bleary-eyed to her window.

She saw pots and plastic buckets cascading down the side of the lower heaps, and two men wearing nothing but their underpants dancing round and round a rice barrel. They chanted like children, 'All fall down.' Mr Chiu, a Chinese immigrant, had opened up his house as a tiny shop. He stood outside it now, still in his nightshirt, distraught, biting his thumbnail. The shop was being ransacked. Third ducked low behind her window.

The men tipped the barrel over, and Mr Chiu cried 'Gentlemen! Gentlemen!', and the rice fell with a hissing sound. The men staggered back from it, laughing. They were soldiers, soldiers for the Neighbours addled on battle drugs, traitor People who had taken off their uniforms. All of this will stop, thought Third, with a sudden jab of military feeling, now that the Neighbours have gone. One of them wheeled around and pointed a finger at the jars in Mr Chiu's window, and the plastic containers burst into flame, belching out black smoke. Mr Chiu gave a little scream and scurried into his house

95

to push the burning jars out of his window with his bare hands. The soldiers plumped down on the rooftop, and woozily began to pull on shirts and trousers. Their feet caught in the cuffs, and they set each other off on fresh bursts of hacking, senseless laughter. The clothes were Mr Chiu's own.

This will not be a day to be out on the streets, Third thought. 'Crow, today we will stay inside. Until everything is settled, and the Neighbours are gone.' Crow seemed to understand. With cowboy cries, the soldiers pushed themselves off down the slopes, tobogganing on their arses, bumping at each level. One of them waved Mrs Chiu's most private garments over his head. Mr Chiu stumbled out through the smoke, weeping, cursing, under the white celebratory linen that was now turning black.

There is no food in the house, Third suddenly remembered. Worse. There is no water. Mrs Chiu was trying to coax her husband back inside. He shouted up at the towers, cursing the People, the harm they had brought him, cursing them for not helping, and he flung a tin up towards them.

Chiu will give us no food, not now, Third thought. I have to go to market. If I go now, while it's early, I may miss the worst of it.

'Stay inside,' she warned the Crow. 'Today is not a good day. Today will not at all be like last night.'

She took her squeaking wagon, and crept down the heap, on the side away from Mr Chiu.

There was an old market that opened early for wholesalers. It had once been well outside the city. The heaps had encroached upon it, shifting. Each day they surrounded it in a different shape. Third came upon it unexpectedly, up and over the roof of a house. She saw the two long sheds in the middle of the square and a mass of black, people in black, rebels, a rebel encampment, and she tried to dart back. Instead, she slipped, and slithered down the side of the house. She landed on the market pavement, with a great clatter, just next to a rebel boy and an old truck.

The boy howled, and spun around. There was a ripple of laughter from the other rebels. Third made a show of laughing, too. The rebel boy did not offer to help her up. He stared at her as if she were a ghost. He had a tattooed face and several wristwatches along one arm and wires trailing out of his ears. Third stood up, smiling. 'Peace of God,' she wished him. 'Grateful praise to long-awaited victors.' The boy's rough country face did not light up with a courteous smile. It stared back at Third, and then shook with a scornful chuckle. He turned back to the truck. It shrank from him, great folds of flesh blinking over the twin lenses of its windscreen.

He climbed into its cab and shouted an order, a wrong order. The truck whined miserably, and twisted in place, refusing to obey. The boy shouted again. This time, the truck did what it was told, and backed up at high speed, into the wall of houses, breaking through the mushroom flesh.

There was desultory applause from the rebels; this boy was not held in high regard. Third saw them, slumped on the stone, sprawled against each other, exhausted, with leaden, unmoving faces. There were girls among them, and they were young, almost children.

The boy jumped out of the truck, slamming shut the metal door that was hung like an earring through its flesh, and it yelped in pain. Inside the broken wall, a woman and two children crouched amid the smells of cold soup and beds. The boy stepped back, his face contorted with rage, and he howled, and he suddenly seemed to fill with light. His eyes glowed with it; it shone orange through the flesh of his cheeks, and lit up the roof of his mouth. It blazed, blinding out of his eyes, and the truck was suddenly engulfed in fire.

'Get out! Get away!' shouted the woman in the house. The truck obeyed; it jumped forward on its wheels and stood still, juddering and coughing in pain and panic. Third ducked away from the heat. Suddenly the truck roared forward across the market square directly at the rebels. They jumped up, or somersaulted backwards out of its way, and it crashed into a wooden support, pulling down a corner of the shed, taking part of the tin roof with it, tipping up and rolling over on to the unliving container that was bolted to the shell of its back. It could not turn over. Its rows of knuckled legs pedalling helplessly, its burning wheels whirring in the air as it steamed and crackled and spat, shivering, whinnying like a horse.

Third began to walk towards a gap between the houses; it was full of hanging laundry; she could hide behind it. She had to leave her wagon behind; it would squeak and draw attention. She began to think she might escape, when she heard the sound of sandals flapping behind her. She went very still and waited. 'City Woman!' a voice said, triumphant.

She turned as they crowded round, craning their necks to see her, with dead, blunted faces. Shadows of smoke wafted across them. Third could smell their sour clothes. They had encrusted teeth and lumps just above the eyelid where parasites dwelt. 'Peace of God,' she said, warily.

'God. Pah!' said one of the boys, spitting at her feet, to a murmur of laughter. Even the spittle was tinged with black.

'I came back to the market, and saw that it was empty, so I am leaving,' Third explained.

'Market!' exclaimed a girl, indignant, and began to strut, hands on hip. 'We have had no market, City Woman, in five years. We had to eat worms. Would you like worms to eat, City Woman?' Then Third understood; this was a brave, naughty girl. She saw again, under the bandanas and weapons and salt-stained black, how young they were, rude children, and she lost her fear. She became outraged.

'I ate worse, girl,' she replied. 'I had to sell my blood. My mother starved to death. I am nearly blind from working in their factories. So don't you spit at me when I give you holy greeting, and call me City Woman, because I am one of the People. And the People show manners and respect!'

Some of them giggled at this old-fashioned display of authority. 'And who is your husband?' challenged the girl, coming closer.

'My husband was a fighter for the People and the foreigners killed him!' The words came out of her without thought; she was bursting with rage, stretched so tight with it that tears oozed out of her, because she finally understood, looking at the foreign weapons, why it was true. 'I am a Country Woman!' she shouted. 'I had to flee here for my life! From the Neighbours!'

This was not what the rebels expected. They looked at each other, scowling and bemused, and scuffed their feet on the stone. 'From what village?' demanded the girl.

Third told her, proudly, fiercely. And for good measure, she cuffed her about the head. The girl did not strike back.

'It's one of ours,' said an older boy, grimly. 'Mata!' he said, which meant 'We have made a mistake.' It was a swear word. He bowed, suddenly, hands held high, and said in another voice, the voice he would have had if there had been no troubles, 'We are sorry, Mother. We have offended without cause.'

'Yes you have!' snarled Third, water shaking itself out of her eyes. The others bowed, murmuring.

'We will escort you back,' the older boy said. 'The streets are not safe. There are too many bad elements. We must deal with them. But we mean no harm to any of the People.' He was some kind of leader among them, with a weary face, his hair tied up in a bun at the back. 'We are fighters for the People, too.' He tried to smile.

Ten of them went with her, pulling her wagon as she stalked on ahead of them, still angry.

'We put out the sheets to meet you,' Third said, flinging a hand up in the direction of the white hangings.

'We expected to be met. We thought people

would cheer us,' said the youngest, and was nudged into silence.

'We sat up all night at fires, singing because you had won,' she told them, bitterly.

She pointed to the fires as they passed them. They skirted mounds of garbage. People lived there too, in shacks made out of garbage. They passed a quagmire of sewage called the Slump. The rebels craned their necks in wonder at how high the heaps had risen, swaying slightly in even this faint morning wind, pinkened by the dawn.

'There are so many!' one of them said. 'It can't be done! What they tell us, eh? We won't be able to.'

'All the real People will leave,' repeated the leader. 'They will leave because they want to leave. The others will not be real People.'

Third was thinking furiously. Leave? All of us? Is that what they mean to do?

Then, against a blue sky, between the Scarecrow and the Fist Raised Towards Heaven, she saw the Crow that Warbled, flying towards them. She gave a little cry and covered her mouth. She knew what was going to happen.

The Crow was singing as it came, a clear morning song, one that praised wifely duties and domestic content. He was greeting her. He was greeting their guests.

'Go back!' Third shouted at it. 'Crow go back! Get away!'

The rebels saw it too, the omen of death. The older boy lurched forward, his face curling with disgust, choking with it. He had seen so much of death that images of it were clear to him. The youngest boy hissed, and picked up a smouldering blade of bone from a fire, and threw it at the Crow. The bird landed in the narrow passageway and hopped towards them, twittering, cocking its head in a sideways question, bouncing towards Third, with whom it was always safe.

'Crow go back,' she pleaded.

'Go back!' the rebels repeated. The Crow hopped up on Third's shoulder and the rebels drew back, and the Crow said hello to them in a cheerful, bobbling note. Then it hopped on to the head of the youngest child. He squealed and went still. The Crow leaned over, upside down, its claws clenched on to his hair, to peer into his face. The boy screamed, and could not move. One of the others swiped the bird from his head, and it fluttered to the ground. The rebels kicked it, and suddenly it let out an ugly squawk of fear, the sound of a real crow.

'He is not Death,' Third was saying, but she could not make the words loud enough. 'Crow! Sing!'

There was a scattering of feathers. The Crow

103

The Crow burst into flame

hopped twice, away from them, and into the air, and its wings made a hearty flapping noise, and it rose up, veering between the rows of hanging sheets, and all the windows were full of the faces of the People, and it was like the Ceremony. The Crow rose up above the sheets, higher than all the towers, to where it always hovered and sang, to where Third thought it would be safe, when the old rebel made a horrible noise, his head full of suppurating memory, 'Uhhhhhh!' as if he were vomiting, and he pointed his finger at the sky, steel clamped around it. Third could follow the tongue of light through the air, see it curve with the nightmare slowness of foreshortened perspective, and her mouth gaped slowly open because she couldn't breathe, and she saw the light flick at the bird, and disappear.

The Crow that Warbled burst into flame. It flew, on fire, orange and red and white, higher than ever before, deeper into the sky. It rose, then dipped, swerving, then found its course again, straining towards heaven. It hung in the sky, still for a moment, and then fell.

It fell, its speed through the air extinguishing its flame. It struck a heap and rolled off it into the air again, thumping into another house, sliding down its side into the box of herbs in Third's window. It flared up again, setting the rosemary alight, scenting the air. There were screams from the People.

Third was still. Third was silent. She wondered very calmly what would happen now that the Crow was destroyed. She was not at all surprised when out of the portal of a house, rocking back and forth down the steps, came a tiger. It sat on the roof of the house below, tamely, and licked its muzzle, and waited.

Everything was muffled, except for the sound of flies. Third's cousin lay at her feet, still in his plaid shirt. The blood was black and congealed now, old. He held up the yarrow stalks towards her.

'But you know how they work,' he said as he had once before, long ago. Third shook her head. She didn't know, not any longer.

Where the rebels had stood, the murderous little Neighbour grinned. His pockmarked face was close to hers, his teeth edged in gold, his eyes gleaming. 'You see? You see?' he seemed to be saying over and over like a bad joke that needs no explanation. 'Go away,' murmured Third. She felt an arm go around her shoulder.

The arm was pale yellow and withered. Third turned and saw her eldest, trusted sister. She was bald, and her face was like an old fruit that had exploded. The eyes had expanded from the sudden heat and burst, the lips had burnt back from the teeth.

'Take off your spectacles, Third,' her sister told her. 'Not now. Slip them off while no one is looking and let them fall. Only City People wear glasses. They will kill you for them. That's right. Slowly. Casually.' Her sister cradled Third towards her, pressing her against the gingham dress. She was still taller than Third, on long stilt legs. 'Oh, I have missed you so much, sister. I have wanted someone to talk to so much. Now we will talk all the time. I will go with you now, and take care of you. We all will. All the Dead.'

Ah, yes, so that's it, thought Third. I see. I see. Crow was like a gate that had broken open. The Dead could come through it. She let her glasses, a scant presence in her hand, drop. Everything was blurred, as if seen through tears. She saw a blurred woman wave her arms, shouting at the rebels.

'It is no good, everyone must leave now,' the rebel was saying.

'But where will we go? How can we leave?' the woman demanded. Quiet, fool, thought Third. They have weapons. And they are crazy.

'Back to the country. Go back to the country so you can be People again, not this City Filth, where you are all whores of the foreigners, with their trash. You go now!'

'But I have to pack my things!'

'You will need nothing. Everything will be provided.'

'My children!'

'Your children belong to all the People. The People will care for them.'

'Madness! Madness!' shouted the woman, realising, staring at them.

'You will all leave before midday,' the older rebel announced. He was a mere wavering of black to Third. 'All leave the city. It is diseased and we are going to burn it!' He threw up his hand, and blasted the sky, and there was a noise like thunder back and forth across it. The People fell silent. They began to be afraid.

Enough, thought Third, and turned, and began to walk.

'Where are you going, Mother?' the oldest rebel asked.

'I am going home, to my village,' she replied, and she thought of her advertisements on the wall, and the drawing of Crow. She had made it look like the Prince.

The rebel grabbed her arm, and turned her around. 'You see?' he challenged the People. 'This woman does what is right. You can too. She is a real Person. Show that you are.'

'Do what they say,' advised Third, glumly, and began to walk again. The rebel walked with her.

'Do not go like that,' he murmured, pressing close. 'Go back to your house. Take some food.'

'There is no food in my house,' replied Third, thinking of the paper flowers.

The rebel pushed a rice ball with a sliver of dried meat wrapped around it into her hand. 'Take this.' He gave her his tin cup. Without looking at him, Third snatched them; without another word, he darted back to the others.

'You see?' Third's sister said, not marching, but sauntering beside her. 'You are charmed. We protect you.' Only the Dead, thought Third, were clearly visible. The living were fading.

It was still quiet, still early. Bands of rebels, chatting, quite ordinary, were wiring up loudspeakers while children looked up admiringly. Somewhere in the distance, a scratchy broadcast voice began. Third could not understand what it said.

Rebels began to go from door to door. Women stood in doorways, listening to them and scowling slightly, holding shut their morning robes, pulling back hair from their faces. Get moving, Third thought, delay will cost you. She heard shouting from inside houses as people disagreed. They took time to pack. Third walked more quickly. There was a crowd in front of a small shop. Third turned sideways through it, and heard the shopkeeper's fat wife say, 'You want it, it costs more today.'

People began to run. Blankets full of things were being lowered from windows. Excited children ran about on the heaps blowing toy horns. Third looked up and saw a man on the very top of a heap. He was rocking back and forth on his heels for balance, trying to coax his house down, on a leash. 'Autumn? Where is Autumn?' a woman called out over and over in panic.

'You won't get out this way,' said Third's sister. Third turned, and began to walk towards the Old City. She cut through stables, where cars slept at night, and climbed up stone steps and out of the treacle-smelling darkness to a paved street.

The Old City was full of people. A woman pushing a baby pram full of tins rammed into her, and without another word shoved the pram into her again, until Third got out of the way.

Third couldn't see. The living jostled past her. In front of shop windows, clothes dummies lay naked and Third thought, with a lurch, that they were bodies. Third looked at the clouds, to rest her eyes. She could see things that were far away, the broad patterns.

She was looking at the clouds, stumbling, when she heard a dull, spreading roar, at once crackling and moist, like a spill of water-melons. It started behind her, to her left, and moved around her in the same way the sound of breaking surf moves

110

along a beach. She turned and saw the heaps collapsing.

She saw a tower pitch forward from its middle, and the houses on top of it separated from each other, scattering, their spider legs kicking as they seemed to almost float down through the air. The main body of the tower nudged another, breaking it in the middle, sending houses somersaulting through the air, spilling furniture, hurtling into other houses, dislodging them, bursting apart. The houses above these, without support, slid helplessly down, other houses still on their backs. It was a contagion, each house linked to another. They collapsed, and broke, and gathered into a massive spreading weight, a roiling wall of flesh. It smashed into the first of the hard stone buildings, rearing up and slapping down on its roof, scraps spilling all over it, and very suddenly it came to a stop. Boom, like that. The noise stopped, and there was a mound of flesh held back by the stone, pressed in layers like the kebabs the Arabs cooked. The sun, through mist, seemed to perch on top of it. A sound came from within it, very faintly, like the squealing of seagulls.

Third turned away, and marched. She walked with her eyes closed as much as possible, humming a song. Opening them, closing them, she saw the dismantlement of Saprang Song in flashes.

She saw a Chinese family burned. They were

The exodus from the city

cheering the rebels, lined up on the roof of an emporium, waving flags, and the rebels burned them, aunts and nieces and grandfathers. Before Third could look away, they were set alight. They stood rigidly within the fire, still holding up infants, like an old family photograph, blackening.

Something stick thin, leaning on a gleaming metal pole, lurched in front of Third. 'Can I take your arm, dear?' it asked. It was a woman. She was wearing a blue hospital coat, and the pole supported a pumping, artificial heart.

'Ask someone else,' Third replied. 'I can't see.'

Something bumped into her, and apologised with two voices. It had wrinkled skin like an elephant, only it was blue: crumpled pyjamas. Two men missing legs were hopping together for support.

Third dimly made out the shape of the hospital building. The rebels were making the patients march as well. Third found herself suddenly in a line of marching things, all down around her knees, hunchbacked, bobbing, and all talking at once, very softly and clearly. 'I am a delicate piece of life-saving equipment,' said a little beige box on muscular, human legs. Another, armoured like a beehive, black, waddled ahead of it. 'I can take over cerebral functions for all blood groups,' it announced in a hushed voice. 'Please treat me with care.'

113

Suddenly a rebel stepped in front of Third. 'You are going the wrong way, Old Woman,' he said.

'I can't see!' exclaimed Third. She could see well enough that the line of machines led to another mound of flesh. There was a shadow on top of it, black. It had a sharp green grin. 'Please treat me with care,' said the little beige box as the shadow brought something, a garden hoe perhaps, down on its head.

'You go that way, to the Bridge,' said the rebel, trying to block her view. 'Across the River, that way there.' Third leaned around him, curious. She wanted to see. There was a white coat talking, a doctor.

'But these things save lives, they can save the lives of your friends, why are you doing this?' wailed the doctor. Without breaking the rhythm of his swing, the shadow brought the hoe down with a crack, on the doctor's head as well.

The rebel grabbed Third's arm and pulled her away. 'She can't see!' he called out to his comrades. Then he murmured, thin lipped, 'You didn't see anything. Did you?'

He led her to a wide avenue that went down the hill to the bridge, and there they were, the People, a dappled mass of them, black-haired heads and many-coloured shirts. Some of them wore coolsuits and hiking boots and rucksacks; some of them carried parasols and twirled them. Some of them sat on the balconies of buildings, as if at a festival, drinking from tins and eating sandwiches. The People, always polite, always patient, talked in lowered voices about practicalities, without complaint.

'Once we are across the Bridge, we will be all right.'

'Sssssh, ssssh, darling, later. We need to save the food for later, all right?'

'Ooooof! It's hot. Why couldn't they wait until spring?'

Third felt her sandal come off her foot. She spun around, but it was lost under a forest of legs. It advanced. 'My shoe! I can't see it. Can someone get it for me?' Third asked. People looked down around their feet, and shook their heads.

'I'm sorry, Mother. I can't see it,' said a City Woman, very prettily. Third could see the blurred back-and-forth motion of her hand, and the wide, white fan with red patterns. Her little daughter looked up at Third in silent dislike. Third could see her black eyes.

'Where are we going, Mummy?' the child asked in a discontented voice.

'You are going, Child,' said Third, unbidden, leaning down, 'to the Unconquered Country.' The little girl buried her face in her mother's side. 'Oh no, you must not be frightened! It is very peaceful there. Everything is as it should be, there.'

'What do you mean?' the mother asked, sheltering her daughter.

Third bowed and made a gesture that enough had been said, and, smiling rather smugly, turned away. It was not for everyone to know. The sun seemed to swell, directly over the middle of the street. The People shuffled forward, a step at a time.

Suddenly the crowd heaved itself up in front of Third. They were on the stone steps of the Bridge. Third climbed them, as if they led to the altar of a temple, feeling a sudden gathering grandness, as if she were being married. Overhead, the great grey workings of the Bridge loomed like a gate. Third could see them clearly. She fixed her eyes on them, as she was carried forward in slow procession by the crowd. Then, at the very hottest moment of the day, under a merciless sun, in the middle of the Bridge, the crowd came to a stop, and did not move again.

The asphalt underfoot was just on the point of melting, a sort of black putty, and Third had to move from one foot to the other, to save the bare one burning. There was nowhere to sit down. The People, pressed together, could smell each other's bodies. Balancing on the railing of the Bridge, holding on to a suspension cable, was a rebel girl, scowling with the heat, blinking. Just below her was the body of a dead soldier. The People backed away from it as much as they could, wrinkling their noses. Third squeezed her way through them, smiling, and sat down next to the corpse. Her knees touched it.

'Hello, Third,' said the corpse. Third looked down and saw that it was Nourisher of the East.

'Hello,' she whispered to him.

'Listen,' he told her. 'You will be on this Bridge for two days. People will die. It is most necessary that you get water. You can survive two days without food, but no water in this heat for two days and you will not be able to stand up, and the rebels will kill you.' He told her how to get water. Third could not accept it at first, would not have accepted it from anyone else. 'Wait,' he said, 'until it is dark.' The rebel girl leant back and drank deeply from a canteen.

Water was a joke at first, to the People on the Bridge. They were so thirsty, and down below, a hundred feet away, was the river. They could hear its roar; they could smell the spray. They drank the last of their warm sticky lemonade. People lost control of their bladders and bowels and could not wash. Infants began to shriek for water. It was only two hours later that Third saw someone jump off

117

the Bridge. He was a young boy. He clung, hunched, to the railing for a long time, before finally letting himself slip off the side. His friends crowded round the edge to look, and then silently turned away.

People began to crawl along the railings to get out. Third nodded up at them, benignly. She was not agile enough to climb, and they shaded her from the sun. For most of the distance, there were no cables to hold on to, and the people see-sawed their arms, until they fell off, landing on the people beneath them: much angry shouting. A man in a brightly coloured short-sleeved shirt fought his way through the crowd. 'Anything to drink?' he kept asking, smiling, perplexed. He had a fistful of paper money. 'All of this, for a bottle of Coca-Cola. Here, look. All of this for you.' A young woman, smiling, shook her head. The man could not believe it. 'Look, what is a bottle of Coca-Cola worth?' The woman still shook her head. 'It could buy you a nice house, a car!' he said, with a yelping, nervous laugh. He looked at Third. 'All my life,' he said, 'I spent it making money.' He moved on. Sometime later, Third saw the money blow past the railings, like leaves.

Surreptitiously, she took the corpse's hand. She wanted to ask Crow if the fire had hurt. She wanted to ask him if he knew that she had made a house for him, and lived the life she would have had if he lived; that she had been happy. But it was difficult to ask such things, and besides, she already knew the answers.

'I came back,' Crow said. 'I could have kept on flying; the flesh had been burned away. But I chose to come back.'

'Boddhisatva,' said Third, realising. Gratefully, she closed her aching eyes and slept.

Suddenly it was cooler, dark. 'Now,' said Crow. Through the girders of the Bridge was a tangle of stars. Amid them, the rebel girl squatted out over the railings, her trousers down around her knees. Third crawled forward with her tin cup. She held it out under her.

The girl squawked, and clenched, and stopped herself.

'Please,' said Third. 'It's only water. It's the only way. There is nothing wrong.'

The girl looked helpless and harassed; finally she had to let go. The water spilled gently out of her; it rang in the tin cup, filled it generously. It seemed such a natural, friendly thing to do, sharing water. Third very elegantly raised the tin cup and sipped it. It was surprisingly cool and mild, only slightly salty. She nibbled her rice ball for a moment, then held it out towards the girl. The rebel hesitated, but was very hungry. Finally, she broke off a piece of it, and gave Third a wisp of a smile.

119

The Bridge

The girl was from Durnang province, to the north. Most of her family were still alive, but scattered. She had never been to school; she had fought with the Ghost Wolf regiment instead. She asked Third why she held the hand of a dead traitor.

'Because he was of the People, once,' said Third. 'There is no difference. The Dead are the living.' The girl did not believe in the Buddha. That was Shinga Iary, she said, Consoling Nonsense. Third repeated the words.

'We must get off this Bridge,' said the girl.

'How?'

'We could just walk out, over them,' said the rebel. 'If there's trouble – pow. Come on.'

Third looked at the People, all lying in orderly rows. 'No,' she said. 'You go. I'll stay.' She watched the girl stumbling out over the backs of the People. Where she passed, there was the wailing of a baby.

Why did I do that, Third wondered. She knelt down again beside the body. She picked up the cold hand. Whose are you? she asked the hand. It looked so small. Did anyone mourn for you? Did anyone love you, like I loved Crow? She looked at the expanse of fallen faces, blue in the moonlight.

There is a part of me that loves them, she realised. That is why I stayed, because they are my People. That is not Shinga Iary. She sat through the night, holding the dead hand.

The next day ground on, hotter and hotter, like a mill. The faces of the People were the faces of the Dead – bloated and unmoving and lopsided, with open mouths. An infant was lapping the asphalt, ceaselessly, with its tongue. Third stroked its head to make it stop.

You are all Dead, she thought, we are all crossing over. The thought made her feel peaceful and at home; all of her friends were Dead. In the city behind, brown clouds of smoke were rising up. In the sky overhead, birds still wheeled on currents of air, and clouds still subtly changed shape, breaking up the light, casting huge shadows through it. Third lay back. I could be a child again, she thought.

'My name is Third,' she murmured to the clouds, 'and I was born in a village called No Harm Can Come . . .'

Her voice trailed off. Why did it seem that there was no point going on? She felt warm, cushioned. She rolled her head and found that her special teacher was sitting next to her.

The teacher was younger than Third now, but she was still smiling. 'Give me numbers,' the teacher said.

Third found that she did not hate her. All of that was so long ago. The woman's face was thinner than Third rememberd, and the smile more uncertain.

You were trying, Third thought, poor thing, you were trying to help.

'I don't have any numbers,' said Third, shaking her head.

'Oh, but you do,' chuckled the teacher, rocking forward on her knees, holding out her hands on either side of her. 'You have faces instead of numbers.'

So I do, thought Third, and smiled back at her. That is what I have. Thank you.

In the sky overhead there was a daystar, moving. The Big People put machines in heaven. High up, there was cold metal and safety. The Big People slid between the stars, it was said, in a network, like a spider's web. That was as close as they would ever get to Heaven. Slide, Third told the Big People, slide and leave, leave the world to us again.

She closed her eyes and dreamed, dreamed of great arches made of white stone in the sky, and the arches made her happy, like being in a temple. They held up the sky and the stars, and there was road, a bridge across a gulf. The boddhisatvas came back along it, out of love, to lead the People. She saw them, wearing gold hats like the spires of temples.

Night. Death. Dawn. Cool breeze, smelling acrid, the odour of burnt tyres, and an ochre sky with a heavy orange sun.

'Now,' said Crow. 'Get up.' The corpse's head had disappeared under a sheen of jelly; and translucent, wire-thin worms twisted in its mouth. 'The worms are the truth,' Crow said. 'They are words.'

'We are numbers,' said Third. Her sister was beside her, and helped her stand up. Third felt very weak; she couldn't lift her feet, so she pumped her knees back and forth to get the blood flowing, as her sister held her arm.

'You have had great fortune, Little Princess,' her sister said. 'You did not starve, or wither. You were loved, but you never became a soldier's wife or a City Person, so the rebels will not hate you. You can lose no one else. You have lived the best life possible in the Land of the Faithful.'

There was a jabbering of orders from far ahead. The People sat up, blinking, prodding relatives, helping them, groaning, to stand up. A mother tried to wake her baby; there was something wrong with the way its mouth hung. The mother shook it, and began calling its name. 'Stand up,' said Third, a hand on the woman's shoulder. 'Take him with you. It is time.'

The ghost numbers rose up, thousands of them, as if ruptured from balloons, reaching up for some reason, some answer. The number of the People. The size of the world.

They found it. Third could see the high white clouds, and there was a bridge across a gulf, and the People were crossing it, Third's sister who was withered, her sister who died in an airport window, an old man Third suddenly recognised from her village. She gave him a friendly wave. There was a man, too, whose face she could not quite see, riding on the back of a tiger.

There came a sudden booming, a crackling. Fireworks? Why should there be fireworks? Third turned in time to see the spires of all the temples on the hill rise up on clouds of dust, like rockets. They were lifted up, and listed to one side, straining towards Heaven, hanging in the air for a moment, and then fell, uninhabited stone. Ah yes, even that made sense. The temples were being killed too, to join them. The temples would be there waiting too, and the villages, and the houses. The houses would greet their families with their cry for the dead.

Third felt something feather-light descend on her back, and something dry and bony wrap itself around her neck, and she felt her mother's face press close to hers. The skull was only lightly covered by a dry crackling of skin. 'I carried you once, daughter,' she said. 'Now it is your turn to carry me.'

And in the sky was a bird made of fire. It burned, leading them, and it sang, a strange sad song that

125

rose up at the end like a question, for everything that had been lost, an orphaned song, for an orphaned people. The bird was not struck down.

'We are going home, child,' whispered Third's mother. 'Third Child, we are going home!'

Afterword

The story of Cambodia is now in danger of becoming a cliché, but it wasn't always so. For many years the story went untold and I spent many years trying to find a way to tell it.

I'm not sure how long ago it was, sometime during the Lon Nol regime in Cambodia, that I saw a photograph in one of the big national magazines, *Life* or *Look*. It was a photograph of a young Cambodian woman in hospital looking at the newly dead body of her young husband. For years afterwards I would find myself imagining her having to walk home alone. In the war-torn city, the temples would be closed, her family would be dispersed. She would have no way to mourn. It wasn't something I could write about – I had never been to Cambodia, or the Far East. I didn't think I had the right to write about it. But the woman kept coming back.

I became friends with someone who had lived both in Laos and Thailand. While in Thailand, he had been researching the content of the delusions of the insane. He had met mediums, he had seen spells cast, he had lived in villages in a modern Asian country that had never been colonised and was determined to stay itself.

Too strong himself for fantasy, he yet said that the magic and the inhabiting ghosts would make a wonderful fantasy tale. I took that as permission to use some of what he had told me. It was not until I realised that my woman lived in a fantasy country – for example, the temples of Phnom Penh were not closed, at least not by the Americans – that the story finally took shape.

When I was a child, I lived in a village, in Canada. Christmas really was a season there. Every house would have a party in turn, and presents would be exchanged then. The children went to school in a wooden frame schoolhouse with a pump well and a bell, that had been built in 1871. When a rabid fox was loose in the village, school closed early and the men of the village went out together, to shoot it. Parents of my friends could remember when wolves would come down out of the north in winter. Now those fields and my best friend's farm have disappeared under shopping centres and tract housing.

I remember seeing the billboards announcing that one day Meadowvale would have a population of 20,000 and being thrilled. I loved the city.

When I was eleven, we moved to Los Angeles, a burgeoning of mansions on hills surrounded by gas stations and liquor stores, a place where even the sunsets seemed to be the colour of old pink Chevrolets. I was there in time to see the very end of American Graffiti and saw it through *Sgt Peppers* armed love and the collapse of the sixties. That bit was fun and sometimes inspiring. But it also seemed to me that what was really meant by culture – an agreed set of values and traditions

– was being destroyed by something bland and corporate and isolating. This story is also about that movement from local to international. It is, in retrospect, about the destruction of culture.

When I finally got to South East Asia, I went to Bangkok and saw Southern California again. I was driven down a divided highway past tacky stucco buildings wilting in the heat, the car windows closed to save the air conditioning.

In the sports club in Bangkok, with its huge pool and ranch-style architecture, Bing Crosby sang *White Christmas*. Outside Bangkok, along the Mitiprahap – Friendship – Highway built by the Americans, there was a row of identical apartment houses. Each one had a huge number painted on its front. Outside the gates of the Thai American Textile Company, stallowners with lampshade hats waited to sell food to the workers. America had just cut its textile imports. 'What kind of friend is that?' a Thai asked me.

On the main streets of Bangkok, choked to a standstill with traffic, concrete dividers had been built down the middle of the road. They had been built to stop American GIs from driving down the wrong side of the road. Not far from the Avon building there was a seven-storey structure decorated with huge red dots. It had no windows. 'It's a massage parlour,' a Thai friend told me, his voice curdling. 'Two hundred girls.' In Patpong, naked boys danced on a stage for the foreigners, hands over their genitals. The metaphor 'rape of a nation' seemed to have been given flesh.

I went to a disco called Rome, and it was full of flashing lights and videos and it was fun, but I might as well have been in New York. I said to someone, 'The Thais were never colonised, but they have been conquered now.'

'They know that,' he said. 'But when you've been here a while you'll see. Everything they do, they make Thai.'

We took a train to the North East of the country and looked across the Mekong river at a Communist capital city. In the border towns were the same large white air-conditioned banks as in Bangkok. We drove through the mountains, being waved on by sullen-looking soldiers at roadblocks. Even in the forest hills in houses made of reed, the television sets glowed. They carried glossy ads for the modern world that used computer graphics. One of them advertised the joys of new concrete houses with corrugated iron roofs.

The traditional Thai house is disappearing. We visited villagers just outside Chieng Mai, and they had torn down their old house to build one of concrete, with white frame windows. It looked somehow mittel-European, suburban. One wall of the sitting room was covered in a huge photograph of an alpine scene with conifers and snow-capped peaks. It was not until later that I realised this new style of building was as distinctively Thai as anything else I had seen.

In the buses, just under the video screens, were garlands of paper flowers and religious tokens. The Shell stations had spirit houses in front of them and the bus drivers beeped when they passed shrines, out of respect.

Afterword

The bus conductors hung out of the doors and shouted destinations, stopping, it seemed, whenever there was a group of people who wanted to get on. Traders would crowd on to the bus too, to sell sticky rice or pineapple chunks to the passengers. The bus gave us a meal of fiery-hot squid on rice. In the towns, there were new hospitals and punk haircuts and bright plaid jackets and T-shirts that said in English 'It's Me!'

As always, what was old was going, and the Thais were not attached to it. They had no need of history to stay Thai. They took us to their national monuments, their ancient ruins, and they looked bored. It was the Westerners who took notes. The Thais want what is modern, and they deserve what is modern, and they will stay Thai.

I took the train back to Bangkok and had another surprise. The train ran beside the Mitiprahap Highway and I saw what I could not see from the road. There were warrens of houses on stilts, over wet ground, with winding, raised walkways between them. I could see over the walls into tiny courtyards and saw family scenes, adults talking, legs folded under them, children running. It looked like the murals of everyday life I had seen on temple walls. There were large unmappable areas of Bangkok where modern roads and buildings could not find foundation.

I had been both right and wrong. The blasting of culture, the homogenisation of the world had gone further, faster than I had thought. But there was indeed something that continued untouched.

133

While I was in Thailand, I also saw something of the screening in or out of refugees. I saw how small the needlepoint of justice is, and how surprising it may be. I saw, for example, that it may be just to deny a refugee family refuge.

I got back to Britain, where I live now, and saw the lines of orderly people going up the escalator at Waterloo station, each of them alone in their heads. I went back to work, writing a PR leaflet about magistrates courts.

All our words have worn out. Democracy, freedom, socialism, economics. They've all become kitsch. They summon up kitsch images. I saw the courts at work and decided that for a while at least, I can cleave to that word justice. It can only be maintained in an artificial environment – in a courtroom powerful enough to preserve its independence, or in a history that with accumulating details sets the record straight, or in a history's bastard child, fiction.

I wrote this story because it didn't seem just that we could talk about America's agony in South East Asia without trying to imagine the agony of the people who live there. And their joys.

This story was written in 1982 and published in a somewhat different version in 1984 by the British magazine, *Interzone*. Many thanks, then, to *Interzone* and to the many friends this story seems to have won in Britain and America.